JULIE'S ODYSSEY: ALPHA AND OMEGA

JULIE'S ODYSSEY: ALPHA AND OMEGA

MYRON EDWARDS

Published by;

RockHill Publishing LLC

PO Box 62523

Virginia Beach, VA 23466-2523

www.rockhillpublishing.com

ACKNOWLDGEMENTS

I would like to thank Lili Panagi of Pan Media, for her constant encouragement and support, Valerie Singleton, a lifelong friend, who has always told me to keep going.

James Hill of RockHill publishing, my publisher, and the brilliant editing skills of Athina Paris, and Mike Clarke my web master.

I would also like to thank the many, many people, who have encouraged me throughout the adventure and to those who bought Book One and Two and those who left comments or reviews.

Finally, I would like to thank my family; my wife Niki and my three children. They have been there in times of great stress and have always told me to keep going.

CONTENTS

DEATH AND CLOCKS

Julie Cole sat alone at the kitchen table sipping her black coffee; she took it extra strong these days. Richard, her husband, was dead; killed during a hit-and-run collision in Cyprus whilst helping his friend Peter. It happened in Paphos, close to Peter's home, and yet, no responsible party had been found. Almost a year might have passed, but coming to terms with grief was something she could not do.

Yes, she had her kids, and both Matthew and Molly were like emotional bricks, offering vital foundations for her mourning. Both strong, sturdy, and resilient, but they too grieved for their Father, while trying to keep their tears tightly under control, so as not to start their Mother's. But inevitably, tears flowed, triggered by the smallest incidents. A word, a comment, even a look stirred them, as the memories kicked in. She glanced at the hot swirls rising from the cup, just another trivial support she leaned on since Richard's demise.

Peter's phone call about the events had been the beginning of a surreal week, as with the passing of days came the slow realisation that Richard was not coming back. Sadly, for all of them, this gradually sunk in.

Since that first day, Julie took to staring at the clock, something she never did before, never paying much attention to the object that had always been there. It had a large wooden case, with distinctive brass hands, and large Roman numerals. It was there, on the mantelpiece, in the living room. Just a simple item that somehow became significant, as it turned into part of her daily routine and gave her something to occupy her thoughts.

She sat watching the hands move back and forth on the face; each simulating her present life. The minute hand ambled, the hour hand even slower, at a crawl until needed, and finally, the second hand rushed through its perpetual circle as it delivered life movements, each depicted in the most simplistic form, tick, tick, tick, its constant rhythm. For Julie, time was all she had left.

Under this canopy of an uncertain future, the Coles lived again.

Sometimes, when no one was around, Julie slinked into her bedroom, opened the wardrobe door, and searched out Richard's chunkiest jumper. She would push her face into the soft fabric, letting her nose catch a breath of his scent. Even now, there was still a remnant that was exclusively him. She breathed it in deep, like a junky on crack, anxious to drag every last sample in; after which she collapsed upon the bed, hugging the jumper to her chest, holding it tight, and wrapping it around her as if he were still inside that precious piece of clothing.

In this position, she fell asleep, just as tears filled her eyes and dried against the pillow. Other times, she talked to herself, as if she were speaking to Richard.

'I ironed your shirts today. Matt has taken to wearing them, since you're not here, and says he likes the feel of them, that they bring you closer to him. I don't know if that's true, but he seems to find them comforting. I am worried about Molly though, she has lost a lot of her sparkle. She was so bright and bubbly while away on her gap year, now, she just looks sad. Richard, I hate you for dying and leaving us like this. Then I stop myself from hating you and hate myself for letting you go and for talking me into another one of your crazy ideas. But I know I couldn't stop you even if I wanted to. That is the hardest part, not controlling your fate and not being there for you.'

In these phantom-filled tantrums, she drifted towards sleep, where her dreams were constantly mixed, the pictures and memories always vivid, but when she awoke, she could barely remember them, all mere shadows. However, there was one she recalled well; the one she had had ever since she was a child, the nightmare that haunted her continuously.

She tried to dream around it, but somehow it latched onto her. It began with a noise, a scratching sound that raked across her head, then came a large translucent ball, that carried within the sound of voices repeating over and over *of course, of course*. As the ball grew bigger, the words became louder, and out of nowhere, a pin appeared and moved slowly to burst the billowing sphere. It grew closer, the words became louder, the pin entered the ball, and she expected it to burst. It never did. The pin just kept travelling through and she woke up. She couldn't fathom the meaning, or know what she should do about it. It had followed her through childhood and now as a woman and mother, it still plagued her.

Most of her dreams included Richard, but recently, they had become tinged with other faces and places, some she recognized, some she did not, with the haunting image of Petra Tou Romiou often playing a backdrop to the scenes unfolding in her subconscious. She saw Peter and Richard, both standing on the shore looking out to sea, as she pushed herself further into the scene. She could almost reach out and touch Richard.

She stretched her hand out, calling to him, saw him turn, and look towards her. Then he turned back as the echo of her voice died in the wind, only to be replaced by another; one she knew well and had hoped would never hear again. Only this time, the voice was calling to her.

'JULIE, JULIE, you must come, you must come. To know the truth, you must come.'

Once awake, she tried to put some perspective on the images, categorizing them by placing them in boxes. She started with the nightmare, followed by the images of Richard and Peter, and finally, Cyprus and the goddess. What was the connection? There must be one, and she knew whatever it was, it involved her.

She had followed the events that had taken place in Cyprus whilst Richard was there, intensely. The sinking of the wedding boat had made all the papers and the significance of that event was made even more personal when the bodies from the disaster were repatriated to the United Kingdom and Richard's own body was among them. She also knew that dying in Cyprus was a quick thing and she would have hated for her husband to be buried there, so it was fortuitous she had the High Commission's help and that of the local coroner and undertaker to do what was described so succinctly by the latter as 'the paperwork'.

Before her were two pieces of paper; the first was the Paphos Police report, one page written in Greek and the other side in English. The words were scant, short, and to the point, the English and grammar hard to follow. She poured over the few sentences looking for clues, or for some reason why he was where he was and who might have wanted to kill him. Because from what she gleaned, she had doubts this was an accident at all. True, her husband had made some people very unhappy, so maybe this was their way of showing just how much.

She read out the first sentence,

'From the marks on the road, it seems Mr Cole tripped. There are roadworks, particularly around the Tombs of the Kings' road, and these works have created traffic problems as some are unfinished. On a dark road, which is where Mr Cole was found, it is possible that he stumbled and fell onto an oncoming car. It appears the vehicle did not swerve or brake but side-swiped Mr Cole, sending him into the road, where he later died. There were no witnesses.'

The other document was Richard's death certificate. Much like the police report, it was short on substance with illegible words scribbled over the paper. She could just about make out trauma, circumstances, and three small letters, RTA. The rest was unreadable as was the Doctor's signature. With this almost threadbare evidence spread before her on the kitchen table it made her even more determined to find out exactly what had happened to her husband. Her grief, for the time being had to be shelved; now, she needed to make plans and the first thing she needed to do was to find Peter.

2

FINDING PETER

*D*etermined to learn the truth, she called the kids together and sat them down by the fireplace in the lounge. She was not sure what to tell them but hoped she would find the right words to assure them that first; she was not going crazy, and second, what she needed to do had some merit, which she needed to do on her own.

Matthew was the first to argue and began packing his bags to leave with his Mother, but Julie calmed him down and smoothed the situation over, with quiet words and a soft brush of his hair with her fingers, as she had always done when he was little.

Molly was more subdued, listening, and saying nothing. She was going to be the tougher of the two, perhaps because she and her Mother were so alike; one could say kindred spirits. She mused over the idea. Personally, she had no wish to travel with her Mother and not to Cyprus, but she saw this trip as two things; one, a chance for her Mum to get away, and two, an escape from the household's atmosphere and its heady, almost tangible grip of grief that clung to the floorboards and hung heavy around the ceiling, as if now part of the house.

It made for an odd sensation knowing there was something

that should not be there, but until they exorcised it, it remained a constant reminder to the family. For that reason, more than the fool's errand she saw the trip to Cyprus as being, she gave her blessing. Finally, everyone agreed that Mum should go, even if there were more than a few missing pieces from this puzzle.

To begin with, no one had either spoken or heard from Peter since the funeral. He edged his eulogy with tears and his words became almost incoherent as he tried to speak of Richard in glowing terms. He had travelled on his own to the funeral, as Sheila, his ex-wife, had shacked up with an oily entrepreneur in some distant land. Oily being the expression he used to describe his adversary, and he did not mean it in the lubrication sense either, more the greasy, slimy version of a business snake. The stranger was the perfect foil for his bitterness towards Sheila, which was all too apparent when the conversation turned to marital matters.

From those snatched moments at Richard's funeral, Julie sensed Peter's deep hatred for Sheila, his words succinct and rich with scorn. Sheila had left an indelible mark on her husband and once a jovial host. Company was the last thing he wanted, as he decided to be left alone, so finding him would not be easy. But determined to discover his whereabouts, no matter the reception, was the first aim.

She had already gone through a few numbers written in Richard's books and emails, but no joy there yet. As she continued searching, she also scanned through the web pages for cheap flights to Paphos, several of which popped up on the screen.

If she could give herself two weeks, perhaps a month, she might delve a little deeper into how Richard had died. After the eighth or ninth number on the list, she lost count.

It was then Matthew came up to her with his mobile. On it was a telephone number and underneath, an address. 'He said if I ever needed to talk, he would be there for me.'

Smiling, she wrote the details before kissing her son's fore-head. Her eyes saying the thank you.

Tomorrow, she would start planning her trip and begin looking for Peter, but first, she needed to sleep. Leaving her coffee, she checked that all doors were locked and bolted and said goodnight to her children, one at a time.

Both were old enough to understand what she needed to do and offered as much support as they could. Molly, always kind, had saved some cash and gave it to her, and Matthew had given her the start she needed. All were on the same page.

PETER HAD DRIFTED FOR A WHILE, before joining the crowd of *Paphos barflies*, most of whom were like him, ex-pats. But included in this company were a few locals, who also frequented the pubs and bars, and likewise were initiated into the group through varying degrees of personal unhappiness. Some had lost their businesses during the recession, some their homes through unscrupulous property developers, who had not delivered on their promises, and others, like him, had lost their wife or husband or family to circumstance and betrayal.

Peter fell into the latter number, having not seen his kids since Sheila left. He wasn't even sure where they were. His phone had rung once a few months ago, and he recognised the number as his daughter's, but it rang off and when he tried to call back the line was dead.

Since returning from Richard's funeral, he had not kept to a routine. He got up when he needed to, drank a Greek coffee, and set off for the nearest pub or bar to join the motley crew of personal disasters, who, like him, found solace at the bottom of a whisky, brandy, or beer glass, depending upon what time of day it was.

Also, he had not heard from anyone since the funeral. The

last text he got from Christoulides was the one with the picture. He kept it, but rarely did he open the message; just another painful reminder of what had happened to his best friend and how he had had no control over the events of his death.

He sunk back into the lounge chair, which, like him, had seen better days, picked up the almost warm Keo beer, and drank slowly while staring into the bottom of the glass.

Around him, four men were wrapped in conversation debating the island's politics, both local and international. Recession and bankers featured heavily in the confused drawl of words that rose in tempo and volume, as the arguments became more vocal. It was a daily ritual for them, with topics which veered between the church and football, but all somehow ended in some type of argument.

Terry, *the elder*, who was the first of the initiates, held court. He had been in a nasty road accident and suffered a broken leg and two cracked ribs. His limp was pronounced, as he rose from his chair, his mouth moving quicker than his hand as he tried to steady himself, 'Fucking bankers broke this place, greedy bunch fucked this place over.' His face turned red, as his blood vessels cooked and his eyes focused on his targets.

Harry, who was much younger, had at one time run a thriving art shop, until the landlord increased the rent and he couldn't find another place to sell his paintings from. He tried online, but advertising and marketing were just too costly. Eventually, he made the decision to burn them, keeping only a handful to give away, and one for himself. He made a big party of it, Souvlaki and Keo, wine and fireworks, as his life's work went up in smoke. Throughout the party, Harry put on a brave face, as both he and his wife, Yvonne, celebrated the end of an era. But if you could see inside, they were hurting badly.

Terry, as the pub's landlord, often let the arguments rattle on, but today he felt he needed to intervene and change the subject. The pub business had been his life for almost eight years; he was ex-army, who settled in Cyprus. The first year or two were good, lots of tourists, entertainment nights, quiz nights, tribute artists, he had them all. He even had bingo once a week, with a top prize of five hundred Euros. That brought in the crowds, but soon, the tourists fell away; the island became too pricey, and the world fell into recession. Greece was first, and Cyprus thought for a while that it would be immune, but it too became the catalyst for financial disaster, which was why these five or six gathered every day to moan, whine, and drink, and not necessarily in that order.

Two of these not-so-magnificent five were Thomas or Tom and the only girl in the group, Samantha or Sam. Her husband had done the dirty on her, running off with one girl from her hair salon, and not just taking the cash till, but clearing out their joint bank account.

Sam was left with the house, two dogs, and a mortgage which she could not pay. She considered leaving the island and returning to the UK, but in England she had nothing either. They had put all they owned into building a life together in Cyprus and her bastard husband, Paul, had well and truly fucked her, and not in the biblical sense. To make ends meet, she tried cutting hair from home but there were never enough customers to go around. One thing Cyprus is not short of, is nail and hair salons or beauty parlours, recession or not. Women must keep up appearances. Sadly for Sam, with no new business to speak of, it became easy to join the *barflies*.

'Two months I've been here…' she said. 'It helps me to see things.'

At forty-five, broke, fast going to seed, and with no prospects on the horizon, it seemed her vision was crystal-clear and usually light-brown.

The last member of this little ensemble was one who should not be there at all, as some vitriol was aimed at him directly. But like a flesh punchbag, he took each sardonic comment without fighting back. He was also the only Cypriot amongst the elite group. Phitos, once the bank Manager at Laiki Bank Geroskipou, now defunct.

Perhaps because it was a small bank by comparison to the larger ones, the comments he got were not as vicious as they could be, more sarcastic than nasty. Yet throughout them, he sat, drinking and smiling, as he tried to do something about his life by sending endless Curriculum Vitae to banks or financial institutions. So far, no one had picked him up and at thirty-five going on fifty-five, he needed a job badly.

In this festering depressive state of drink and despair, Peter resided.

JULIE BEGAN CLEARING the things she needed to do and found a flight at a good price. Easy Jet into Paphos; no frills, no food included, and not too much leg room. Still, it was a seat and she needed to be in it. She was content as she had also booked her first night at one of the hotels in Kato Paphos, the *Sun Spot*. Nothing elaborate, just somewhere where she could rest and relax, before she set about her task.

She thought about calling Peter, but that might scare him off and she was uncertain in what state he found himself or what he might be doing. But she had his address now, so she hoped he was still there, as she definitely wanted to see him face-to-face. Besides, Paphos was not a big place, it would not be too difficult to find him. Still, she would call him first in case he had moved.

THE SUN SANK into the clouds as Peter shuffled back to his apartment. Still with all his faculties intact, he hoped he was not getting used to it, as the drink he had consumed was not having much effect on him today. This was a dangerous sign, one he would have to be aware of.

But unbeknownst to him, the life he had tried so hard to forget through his daily excursions and membership of the *barflies*, was about to emerge again and with it, a relentless pursuer who would not take no for an answer.

THE JOURNEY

Molly got up early to say goodbye, but the conversation was stilted, few words exchanged, and she returned to bed. It was like that all the way to the airport as well; Matthew barely spoke.

Julie looked out of the window, recalling her first drive with Richard on their way to Cyprus and how it had all gone so smoothly. But today, traffic was stop, start, and stop as the car laboured along through the rush hour, before finally easing, allowing Matthew the chance to change from second to third and fourth. She checked her watch. The plane was due to take off in three hours; they had time. Still, her nerves frayed as they drew closer to the exit for the airport. 'When we get there, just drop me off. Don't come in, the parking is crazy money, so I'll go straight to departures, okay?'

Matthew knew he could not argue, nodded his accord, and as the sun began to poke its way across the windscreen, he reached for his sunglasses.

Julie took them from him and wiped the lenses with a tissue, before handing them back.

'Thanks,' he needed to tell her something but could not find the right words, instead, he gave her some advice. 'Please be careful.'

As the vehicle rounded the turn for the departures, Julie took his hand and squeezed it. 'I will. And you look after your sister, she needs you more than ever now.'

He pulled over into the unloading bay and on cue, a heavy-set warden bedecked in neon-yellow stripes around his hat and jacket walked towards them. Julie got out quickly, moved swiftly to the back of the car, and grabbed her suitcase. Matthew joined her, hugged and kissed her, then rapidly made his way back to the driver's seat, just as the warden was in almost touching distance of the bonnet.

As the car pulled away, Julie turned and swerved to avoid a carousel of trolleys being pushed by a dark-skinned airport assistant. She hurried through to departures, then looked back as the sliding doors swished behind her. Matthew was gone.

Swiftly, she dodged through the packed departures hall towards Easy Jet's check-in area, and scanned the electronic board until finding her flight number. Ahead stood a line of about fifty people with various suitcases and bags, which they pushed and tugged as they moved closer to the counter. In fits and starts, one by one, or four by four family members moved away from the desk. She checked her watch again, then the line. Soon, it would be her turn to answer the obligatory security questions as the people shuffled along.

The plane was delayed for thirty minutes but when eventually airborne, the Captain assured them they would still land on time, with the temperature in Paphos in the high twenties. She had forgotten how hot Cyprus could get and how Richard had been burnt by the sun at Aphrodite's Rock. She closed her eyes, the hum of the engines her only tune as she shifted awkwardly in the tight seat to gain more comfort. Her fellow companion, a small, thin, Greek-looking man in his fifties, slept beside her, his pillow scrunched tight against the edge of the seat.

As the aircraft banked, Paphos' lights came into view.

Her Greek neighbour nodded as he pushed the pillow under his seat, redid his seat-belt, and smiled before crossing himself. He then resumed his posture as he leaned inward towards the window. The crew busied themselves with final landing instructions and the plane edged down. The loudspeaker repeated its earlier announcements, only this time, the stewardess hurried. The plane landed with a sharp bump, the roar of the engines in reverse inspiring spontaneous applause. Something Julie had never quite understood about Cypriots. Were they thankful to be home, that they had landed safely, or a combination of both?

Unlike some of her fellow passengers, she waited to appropriate herself of her bag from the overhead compartment. The thin Greek man was anxious to get past her but he too waited more out of necessity than manners as the gap between her and the aisle was small. Eventually, the plane stopped, bags were retrieved, doors opened, and the passengers disembarked. The last time she had been here coaches had been waiting to take them to the terminal. This time, they walked across the concourse and straight into the terminal. Once inside, she was greeted with a display of Cypriot scenes displayed on a LED sign; most, paying some reference to the Cultural capital in 2017. Naturally, Aphrodite's image was resplendent throughout the building, and so were the Rocks. One set of pictures showed Petra Tou Romiou without the rocks in the background, whilst the follow-up picture showed them returned to their natural state. Richard's influence was everywhere, his legacy living on as visitors emerging from their aircraft could clearly see for themselves.

Julie moved into the European citizens' line, waited her turn, approached, and handed over her passport.

A smartly dressed young female security officer sat impassively behind the glass wall, her face barely visible, and surrounded by a set of computer screens. She took the passport and in what seemed an after-thought, called over the supervisor who stood behind the glass wall box. There were a few hushed Greek words between them, and even before the book was opened, she leaned forward. 'Please wait here, Mrs Cole.'

The recognition of her name meant only one thing, this would not be over quick.

'Follow me, please.'

Julie picked up her bag and followed the man, who was more than a little overweight but kept a healthy stride as he marched off in front of her at a good pace, making it difficult to keep up. The man turned and addressed a policeman who stood in front of a door marked SECURITY. Her anxiety shot up a notch. This trip was looking like it could be over before it began.

The door opened and the bare essentials of an office greeted her; a wooden desk, chairs, and a computer screen, plus an array of official-looking forms and documents stacked neatly in piles upon the desk and the obligatory pictures of saints and icons. She was invited to sit inside, then the door closed, and they left her alone.

Swiftly but quietly, as if to enter unnoticed, a gentleman opened the door and was beside the desk. 'Mrs Cole, forgive us for detaining you, but as you no doubt appreciate the situation with your husband's sudden demise, it has left us in a state of some confusion. Naturally, we wish to be as helpful as possible during your stay here.' He said apologetically.

He was a short man, smartly dressed in a tailored grey suit, with a white shirt, and gold cufflinks. She guessed he was in his forties but possibly younger. His face was well tanned, with a tidy, almost black beard covering most of his face. She watched the bright blue eyes, then glanced at his fingers and noticed he didn't wear a wedding ring or jewellery, just the gold cufflinks.

'My name is Marios Lakis, the liaison for the Ministry of Internal Affairs. I was involved with the repatriation of Mr Cole to the UK, which is why I wanted to speak with you this evening…'

His accent, like his appearance, was impeccable; he did however have a slight trace of Greek in the inflexion of the words, but apart from that, his delivery was straight from Kings College.

'I need not tell you how much the island has changed since you and Mr Cole first came here. But with his untimely death, in shall we say suspicious—and that is my opinion—circumstances, is a question that many on this island want answering. No doubt you do yourself. I can tell you, Mrs Cole, we have turned this island upside down trying to find whoever did this but have found nothing. If your visit here is to try investigate, shall we say, the accident, I tell you now, please don't, there is no more you can do.'

Looking straight at him, she knew the words were a warning to not ask too many questions. 'Thank you, Mr Lakis, I appreciate your concern.' Her Boston tone stressed her words.

The man looked surprised.

'But you are mistaken, I am here for Mr Shaw. Since Richard's death… we are not afraid to use that expression. Since his death, Mr Shaw has been in a state of flux, shall we say? So, I am hoping my visit will bring about a change in his welfare and that we can mourn together, something we could not do before. I see it as a personal matter.'

'There is nothing personal when it comes to the security of this island, so I must take precautions whenever necessary, so as not to upset the balance. I am sure you appreciate that. Your presence, therefore, must be low key, we do not want the media stirring things up again.'

Julie said a little indignantly. 'Mr Lakis, Mr Shaw is my friend, who is going through a very rough divorce. I thought the least I could do was come give him moral support, and grieve with him.'

'Yes, we have knowledge of this man. He used to fly tourists, and made some unscheduled flights. One, I hear, got him sacked.'

'Oh, I didn't know that.'

'Yes, Mrs Cole, like so many here, he lost his job. A few hundred others also lost theirs when the incident at the Rocks happened. You can't take people to Aphrodite's Rock when there isn't anything to see, can you? But, miraculously, they re-appeared and we now have more tourists than we can cope with, and our bid for the Cultural City of Europe; the Rocks lending more credence to that bid. The place is steeped in legend, myth, and magic. Mr Cole made us all realise that.'

'I suppose so, and I am sorry, I knew nothing about this.'

'So, since you have come to support your friend, let me detain you no further. Do you have transport? Your luggage has been retrieved and is waiting for you in duty-free. I will have a car take you to wherever you need to go. How long do you think you will stay with Mr Shaw?'

'A few days, no more than a week, perhaps ten days. I know he has some things to sort out. Property and—'

'Splendid. Please take my card if you need anything while you are here, and do not hesitate to call.'

'Thank you, Mr Lakis.'

'It is my pleasure, Mrs Cole, and may I say, welcome back to Cyprus. I hope your stay will be a pleasant one and not too upsetting.'

Taking Lakis' hand, she stood up. His handshake was clammy, which was a surprise in someone so articulated and well-dressed. If she needed proof, the handshake was it. This was a man not of his word.

Lakis handed Julie her passport, opened the door, and the two walked back out into the corridor where her case stood at the end by the *Customs* and *Nothing to Declare* desks.

She collected it and quickly made her way into the arrivals hall.

A young man dressed in black walked out of nowhere, stepped forward, and grabbed her case. He wore a crisp white shirt, black tie, polished black shoes, shiny white teeth, and closely cropped hair. Once again, she was in pursuit of a man; only this one had her luggage.

Lakis stepped back into the office, took out his phone, and pressed the keypad. The phone rang twice. 'Some news, sir. Julie Cole has arrived in Paphos. She says she's meeting with Mr Shaw… I see, yes, of course… yes, I will take care of it personally. Yes, I understand… nothing else, no… thank you… I will be in touch… goodbye, sir.'

THE YOUNG MAN ferried Julie towards a sleek black Mercedes parked outside the arrivals hall and introduced himself as Alexis, while opening the door to usher her into the back seat.

Sitting comfortably on leather, she watched through the back window as Alexis busied himself putting her suitcase into the trunk, then climbed in, clicked his seat belt on, and checked his mirror to see her staring back at him.

'Some music, Madam?'

She leaned forward. 'It's Julie, not Madam or Miss or Miss Julie. I'm not some girl off a southern plantation. Just plain Julie, okay?'

'Okay, Julie, but there is nothing plain about you.'

She smiled at the young man's attempt at flirtation while the car headed towards the main road. Noticing there was little traffic about, she leaned forward again and told him. 'I want you to take me to the Tombs of the Kings' Road before we go to the hotel.'

'But… Mr Lakis has arranged a reservation at the Alexander

The Great; said you would be more comfortable there than at the place you booked. That room has been cancelled and I am to take you to the Alexander.' Alexis' Greek accent became more pronounced and a look of worry came upon his youthful face.

'No, Alexis, Tombs of the Kings first. That's what I want to do.'

'If you are sure… and as long as you don't tell anyone. I can lose my job if they find out.'

'You won't lose your job, just take me there, please.'

Her stance meant there was no point in arguing and as he reached the crossway of the main road, he turned the vehicle left and into the country road, following the signs to Geroskipou. At the end of the town was a large roundabout that crossed over into the Tombs of the Kings' road and he drove through the bumps cautiously, so she would feel no discomfort. Most of the town was in darkness, only one or two café bars and tavernas showing their lights.

Julie looked through the side window. Several of the shops were closed and not just for the night, some had For Sale signs, whilst others were boarded up. The recession was biting hard, even in the tourist area.

The Mercedes crossed over the roundabout and into the Tombs of the Kings road, then slowed down as a policeman hunched over his motorbike kept a tight grip on his hand-held speed camera. They passed a big church on the left and the new Mall, before burrowing their way through to the start of the roadworks.

Julie sat up and caught glimpses of the bright neon signs for the restaurants and fast food offerings, and the more sedate lighting of the bars and Greek taverns; most of which seemed relatively busy. The car progressed past the outlets until the road became slimmer, forming a single line of traffic as the roadworks multiplied. Continuing to gaze out, she noticed a section that appeared cordoned off, with one or two signs protruding out into the road. Behind them, she glimpsed a small wooden cross and two piles of what looked like dead flowers lying next to it. 'Alexis, can you please turn around? Up ahead is a garage, turn there and stop. I will get out, there is something I want to see.'

Alexis sped up, pulled the Merc into the garage before spinning back onto the road, and travelled for about a thousand yards before stopping, leaving the hazard and headlights on. 'Julie, the road is not safe. There is not much light and the cars can't always see you, please be careful.'

She swung open the car door. Alexis was right, there was little room to manoeuvre, but she picked her way to where the cross stood. It was easy to see how Richard could have been hit by a passing car in the oppressive darkness. There was no path to speak of, and she had no doubt of that now she had seen it. Alexis would have to navigate the narrow roadway carefully, as it was precarious. But this knowledge still begged the question. What had Richard been doing here, and why?

PETER ENJOYED STROLLING along the harbour walkway, up towards the fort, and back again. He passed restaurants serving *catch of the day*, such as the Pelican, once famous for the bird that used to frequent its front, but was now long gone. Or he stopped at Hobos and had one dose of neat ice-cold Zivania to crack his malaise before he was ready for the next stage of his journey, which was becoming a little harder to do each time. After his drink, he walked towards the harbour wall, and stopped at the jetty where boats left from for their pleasure cruises.

In front of him was a hand-painted sign, RIP. Once, this was an advertising board but now, in its place, were pictures and fresh flowers arrayed in glass cabinets. This was what he saw on his nightly homage to those whose lives ended so tragically on the wedding boat last year and to whom he felt somehow attached.

Memories of those last days haunted him and he could almost feel Richard standing with him as he bowed his head reverently to the departed. Sometimes, he stared at the pictures; the shadowy faces trapped behind glass, staring back. All were dressed in their finery, next to pictures of the boat bedecked in wedding balloons and tinsel, showing her proudly sailing out at sea with the guests on board waving from her decks. A small group of onlookers or just the curious often waited with him; some took out their phones, clicking discretely. As if these images would ever make it inside their Facebook page.

On one occasion, he remonstrated with an individual, whose fascination for the morbid became too much when he tried to take a selfie standing beside the case. The fracas was over in a few seconds after a couple of stall holders emerged on the scene with the embarrassed tourist taking great strides towards the car park. But tonight, there was no one like that. He paid his respects and moved away back down the harbour walk towards his apartment.

Dodging traffic, he crossed the road to head downtown and took out his keys as he approached the entrance. The light above attracted a few insects, and he looked up while pushing the key into the lock. Entering the building, he climbed the stairs whilst holding onto the bannister and switched on the light to apartment number eighteen.

Inside, his first move was to scurry to the fridge and pull out a small Keo. He opened the beer, sinking each drop more urgently than the last, and then, still drinking, pushed himself into his one-room bedsit and sank onto the sofa-bed, sipping slower than before. With one move, he hit the TV remote button and an old 90s film flickered on the screen. In front of him was a small pile of bills, unopened. Placing the almost empty bottle on top of the letters, he flicked through the channels, seeking something more interesting than the usual Cypriot soaps.

He settled on National Geographic and the Wilds of Russia. A far cry from his alcohol-induced sweaty shirt and shorts he was wearing. *I could do with a visit to the bleak winter of Russia. It would make a pleasant change.*

4

THE TEMPLE OF NECROMANTEION

Fenchurch Street Station in the City of London is a busy commuter station serving the travelling needs of the public who usually work near and around the area. Close by, stands the Tower of London. Dating back to the days of William the Conqueror in the eleventh century, it has stood for over a thousand years as a place of infamy, treason, executions, torture, and betrayal. Ironically, one of the entrances accessed only from the River Thames is called 'Traitor's Gate.'

In and around Fenchurch Street are many different buildings of all shapes and sizes, some dating back to the Tudor times. Intermingled with these smaller enterprises are the giants of economy, places like Lloyds of London, famous for its insurance business, or the shipping offices of P&O whose fleet of fabulous cruise liners still sail today. The city's landmarks tower above the streets; icons such as the immensely popular and staggering architecture of the 'Shard' or the cutely-named 'Gherkin Tower', just two of the cash-grabbling attractions that the metropolis offers its guests.

Yet amid this hive of commerce and business and all the conglomerates of the good 'old square mile', one building remains almost aloof and obscure, its rooftop only visible at certain angles, as it folds into a triangle that pinches the skyline.

Most people are oblivious to this edifice, except those who use it. For them, it is a rare and distinct privilege to enter the premises as they are part of a group whose clandestine motives are etched indelibly in the mystique of darkness. They slip in unnoticed, as commuters hurriedly rush past in pursuit of their train or next meeting.

The façade looks almost bland, but as they enter, two large oak doors open and the participants cross the threshold onto the mirrored marble floor which echoes to the sound of their footsteps. Together, these chosen few make their way through the corridors to enter a large conference room of sorts. However, this furniture is much older, with heavy wooden chairs positioned around the polished surface of an oak table—the same wood as that of the door. In the centre of the table is a small glass vase, filled with dead flowers, the water unchanged, and green in colour.

As the guests enter the room, the first voice speak out. 'Good to see you again, Dracos, it has been too long.'

Dracos nodded in acknowledgement and remained standing.

He was a tall, imperious-looking individual with huge, broad shoulders and a barrel of a chest. His hawk-like gaze surveyed the guests one by one as they entered the room; guarding was his natural forte. Above piercing black eyes was a small scar just beneath his right brow, a souvenir of a past conflict. His age was difficult to guess, perhaps forty, or older. He was dressed in a black suit and tie, while the other participants donned black one-piece capes.

'Do you know why we are here?' A young woman with shimmering black high heels and coiffured black hair turned to the man standing next to her.

He was much older and looked distinctly unimpressed as he

kept glancing at his watch. He needed to be somewhere else, not here, that was plain from his body language.

Nobody acknowledged the woman.

Dracos spoke to the assembly. 'Take your places behind your chair, he will be here in a moment. No one is to speak. Unless spoken to.'

They positioned themselves inside and around the room, the sombreness of the occasion summed up by the dead flower in the frosted glass vase, perhaps a slight attempt to disguise the coloured green water.

The door at the end of the room creaked open, a thin bony hand gripped the edge, and pushed it ajar. As a figure entered, the present company came to quick attention.

He wore a crimson jacket edged with black stripes—which looked too big as he ambled in—and black trousers tucked into highly-polished red boots. His bright green eyes, like a chameleon's, moved from side to side, checking the attendees, making sure they paid homage to his presence.

Heads bowed, no one daring to look upon the weathered skin.

He grimaced a sarcastic smile, which accentuated his emaciated body and the creases in his paper-thin cheeks. 'Sit,' his deep voice said, belying the portrayed decaying frame.

The dozen or so attendees sat obediently in their chairs, shivering inwardly, as each shuffled into a position that allowed their eyes directly onto him.

Dracos stood closest to the man. 'You will all swear your allegiance.' He ordered.

They stood as one again, each taking the hand of the other and holding it. Their voices cut the silence. The words to the uninitiated would horrify the listener. 'Oh, Master of Death, accept me as your servant. To serve only you and to worship only you. To acknowledge you as supreme ruler of death and the after-life. Take my soul, to do as you please with it, and make me worthy of you, Master of my Death, My Lord Hades.'

Acknowledged to his liking, Hades slipped onto his throne-like chair at the head of the table, then nodded for the others to do likewise.

All sat down, save Dracos who stood motionless, then said. 'The temple of Necromanteion is in session.'

A grimace cut across Hades' face and with his left hand, he motioned Dracos to sit. Hunched over the table, he leaned forward to speak, his voice deep, his words delivered slowly. Those closest to him could smell his fetid breath. 'I have spoken with the Oracle and she has told me my brother seeks the blood of the Gorgon. This can mean only one thing, he seeks resurrection. This will put this Temple in direct conflict with my brother, but it is a contest I do not wish to indulge in, I alone must have the Gorgon's blood with it.' He paused and glanced across at the man nearest to the oak doors.

At the bottom of the table, the participant twitched uncomfortably and looked down at his watch again.

Hades snapped upon the wandering attention instantly. 'Are we keeping you?' He said while looking straight through the man.

'No, sir, forgive me, it's just that I have a train to catch.'

'A train to catch. Hmm,' The sarcasm was almost visible in Hades' eyes. 'Well, don't let me keep you...'

'Thank you, sir, I mean... my Lord,' The man stood up nervously and moved his chair back.

Hades watched with no emotion. 'Before you go, I want to ask you something.'

'Yes, my Lord.' His body shook from inside.

'Do you know what it is like to die?'

The room fell into a hushed silence as the man's breathing became shallow.

Dracos reached inside his jacket, placing a hand on the scabbard of his knife. When Hades lifted a small finger to signal it was not needed, he returned his jacket to its position.

Tension built in the room as Hades waited for the reply. None came as the man bowed his head.

'Of course, you don't, you're not dead. YET.' He emphasized. 'Allow me to explain. I will elaborate in the ancient ways so it is easy to follow. Here in this sacred ancient temple, we perform certain rituals when called upon to do so. Naturally, as custodian of the Underworld I am involved in the process more than others. You see, the spirits of the dead do not just lie waiting for their calling.'

The man's face dripped perspiration, his eyes opened wide, and he clutched at his chest; the internal pounding beat making him gasp as he rocked back onto the polished table. Gradually, his throat tightened, his breathing stifled, and he could not utter a sound. As the robe slid away, it left him in his business attire and he felt tension in his muscles, as if they were being squeezed tighter, his body being crushed slowly. All his clothes slipped from his body and he stood totally naked in front of the assembly.

'When the body dies, as you will soon know for yourself, we place you in the earth.' Hades continued, his words crumbling the human before him.

Fear ran around the room as the others watched in horror.

One by one his fingers cracked, then snapped, and finally broke, sheer agony etched across his face as the digits pulled together into one pulsing mass of bloody flesh. His body shook uncontrollably and his ribcage contorted as he was squeezed even tighter. As the movement pressed further into his body, his head followed the same pattern as his ribs. The skull fractured, piece by piece cracking open. His hair or what was left of it congealed with the brain matter that oozed from the bone fragments littering the floor. How he was not dead yet was purely down to Hades, stressing his sheer torment and pain, keeping him from falling and letting him die, his legs propping up his now disintegrating body.

The only screams came from the terrified woman, whilst the rest silently witnessed the unfolding horror.

Whatever breath was left in the man became pressurized as a last guttural gasp left his body. Blood and body fluids spilled across the floor as his frame dropped into a pulsating mass of flesh, bone, guts, and sinew, creating a line along the wooden floor. The human offal and blood congealed, to form a single line of human sludge.

Beneath the mess, a portion of the wooden floor slid open, a drain pipe appeared, and the goo plopped into a sewer. The stench billowed into the room, as a mix of blood and organs slewed down into the pipe. As the fluid drained away, the pipe closed, and the floorboard returned to its former position. The odour persisted for a few seconds more until the pipe and floorboards sealed shut again.

Hades moved closer to peer down at the remaining sliver of fluid. 'As you observed, the body goes through the pipe, makes its way back into the earth, after gradually being teased and sloshed about through sewers, and then into the soil. After which, it will travel wrapped in its soul. It releases the soul from the earth at the same time as the mess you saw before you. Finally, they join up in a biological, chemical, and spiritual reunion. As it travels through the fissures and cracks of the land, it is necessary for it to be thin and precise. We can't have bodies getting stuck in pipes or sewers, can we?'

The occupants of the room tried to stifle a smile.

'Finally, he will arrive in the Underworld, where his soul will be stored for all eternity whilst his messy torso or what is left of it is emptied into the great River Styx. A rare privilege, one would say.' Hades moved to the empty chair and placed his hands on the back of it. 'Our friend here has just begun that journey.' He studied the room's congregants.

Most were trying to contain the bile stuck in their throats.

'Dracos, some brandy for our members, please. I am sure they must be thirsty after such a performance. Thereafter, we shall get down to business. I will leave it to you, Dracos, to make the arrangements for our friend and his family. The usual story will suffice.' He looked down at the floor. 'And all because he had a train to catch. What a pity he missed it.'

What was left of the hideous spectacle was the tiniest fragment of a businessman's black woollen suit, which stuck between the floorboards.

Hades moved to the woman, took her hand, and pulled the robe from her. With his bony fingers, he tore the rest of her clothes off piece by piece. The marvel of death always aroused him.

Naked, she lay down on the table, and let the King of the Underworld rape her, taking his pleasure. The others watched, sipped their brandy, and waited their turn.

5

A SURPRISE AWAKENING

*A*s they drove towards the hotel, it gave Julie enough time to start thinking of her next move.

Alexis kept his eye on the road, but his attention was squarely on his passenger through the rear-view mirror. He watched as she scribbled quick passages in a notepad, before scuffling them into her handbag. Then, as if in an after-thought, taking the pad out again to write more. He could only hazard a guess as to the notes, although he was fairly certain the stop they had just made was the catalyst for the scribblings.

As they arrived at the five-star Alexander Hotel, Julie peered through the window at a large imposing glass building with security gates.

Alexis flashed the lights, the barrier rose, and the car entered the property, pulling smartly into the parking area, where the concierge was waiting.

An impeccably-attired uniformed man who was used to greeting Presidents and Kings welcomed Julie, his face beaming a smile that was so rehearsed, even the veins on his forehead seemed in unison. His eyes remained bright, even though it was late, but for most people in his position, tiredness and boredom had become the norm. Shrugging lethargy away, he offered a resplendent smile. 'A warm Alexander the Great welcome, Mrs Cole, we are delighted to have you here. I hope your stay will be a very pleasant and fulfilling one.'

'Thank you, Mr…'

'Paniakos, Mrs Cole. As it states on my name tag, Head of the Concierge Department.' And to emphasize the importance of his role, he pointed to said badge.

'Forgive me, it's been a long day.' Her Boston accent emerged again. It seemed to do so whenever she was embarrassed or felt awkward.

'Understandable.' His English was eloquent and delivered with such precision that no one would ever misinterpret his meanings. 'The Key Porter will take you straight to your room, I have made reception aware of your personal details. Mr Lakis made sure they would not detain you upon arrival, though I thought you would have been here before now…'

Alexis looked at the floor, his admonishment non-verbal.

'But I know the traffic is particularly heavy with these infernal roadworks. Come, let us not dwell on this, I wish you a good night. Is there something I can get you from room service; a light snack, coffee, or a nightcap perhaps?'

'Thank you, no. Wait… I will have a frappé, two sugars, and half and half.'

Paniakos smiled. 'Coming right up. You are in suite Four.'

Before she could confirm his words, the Key Porter had her cases in his hands and was outside the lifts. She followed attentively.

The porter pressed button 4 and the lift ascended quickly and noiselessly. It took mere seconds to reach the fourth floor and she followed on. As they turned a corner, a set of white and gold doors opened before her.

She stepped inside and the first thing she saw was the bed. It was enormous, either King or Queen Size. She couldn't decide as she sat on the *Goldilocks bed* (not too hard and not too soft, just right).

She looked straight ahead at the amazing glass windows that seemed to stretch the entire length of the wall as the Key Porter opened them slowly, revealing a balcony which presented an entire vista of the bay outside. To the right, the brighter lights of Paphos revealed its parade of seashore bars and shops, and to the left, were the bays of Geroskipou, where illumination twinkled like crushed tinsel, flickering and indistinct.

On the horizon, two small white lights dotted the dark blue waters, belonging to two fishing boats which bobbled and drifted across, awaiting their catch. The sea breeze caught the net curtain, and she closed the door behind her.

Turning, she saw the Key Porter standing almost at attention and reached down to pick up her purse to give the man a tip.

He politely nodded his head.

She returned the money to the purse, bid him good night, closed the door behind her, and locked the door, not once but twice. A handwritten envelope sat on the coffee table, addressed to her. She opened it.

'Welcome, Mrs Cole,

I trust you will enjoy your time with us and if I can be of service, contact me.

Christos Paniakos.'

He had not put his title, leaving it as a personal note, not one of business.

Sitting on the bed, she realised that for the first time that day she was alone. She kicked off her shoes, pulled off her top, skirt, and lay back in her underwear, then pulling those off, she lay naked on the bed, feeling free. She sat up slowly, looked around at the lavish décor, and slipped on her complimentary slippers before parading into the bathroom.

It was an enormous room, yet warm, cosy, and inviting. In the centre stood a Jacuzzi, just waiting to be filled. There was also a separate power shower and a Victorian-style bath. The décor was pure white and the glass mirrors shone from all four corners, mirroring her reflection from three hundred and sixty degrees. She would wait to use the Jacuzzi, but she was ready for the power shower.

She stepped in and the water flowed instantly at room temperature. It hit her skin in several spots at once, as six precisely positioned jets fizzed warm water at her body, then began turning hotter with every advancing second. Invigorated, her skin bristled and reacted as the positioning of jets pulsed and probed, the heat and sensation from the power spray bringing on natural stimulation, revitalising her, so that a new pink hue appeared all over.

She moved her head under the top shower point and let the water do its work, washing away not only the arduous journey but also cleansing her face and hair. She reached down for the shampoo and bodywash and lathered herself from top to bottom, adding an extra dimension to the pleasure. She was finally coming alive again.

Naked, she found sleep easy at first, but soon, the troubling dreams began and she found herself plunged back into unfathomable scenes. First, Peter's face appeared, then was quickly replaced by Mr Lakis. And throughout the visions that voice kept calling, 'Julie, Julie, you came. There is little time, wait for me, wait for me.'

The voice died down as quickly as it began, as if disturbed. Then, there was darkness; a deep, dank feeling in her head, heavy and weighing her down as if she were being pulled somewhere. It was then she saw it, the box; a square glass container covered in mirrors, its shimmer cutting through the darkness. She felt compelled to draw closer and place her hand on it. The lid was almost open, but a gigantic hand slammed it shut. She awoke sweating, her face dripping perspiration. The pillows and sheets had absorbed the nightmare.

She awoke quickly, made her way to the bathroom, and stepped into the shower, turning on just one tap; this wash would not be as dramatic as her first encounter. After towelling herself dry, she picked her way through her opened suitcase. Quickly climbing into briefs and bra, she doused herself in deodorant, then checked her phone.

Only one message, which she had received the night before, having announced her arrival to Molly and Matthew. She glanced at the time, 8:30 am; there was a two-hour difference, so they would not be up yet. She walked over to the glass windows and pulled back the net curtains.

The Mediterranean was in its full glory, white horses riding towards the shore on a carpet of foaming blue waves, each one balanced in time until another took its place. Julie watched as the sun christened the water with its daily blessing of warmth and recalled the first time she and Richard witnessed those same waves washing ashore from their balcony in Limassol. She closed the curtains and dressed quickly, jeans, red top, purple cardigan, and a pair of walking sandals. She applied just the faintest makeup and some lippy. Then taking her key, she left the room with her bag dangling over one shoulder, phone in hand, and most importantly, a map in the other. Alone in the lift, she descended to reception without interruptions to make her way into the breakfast room.

A smartly-dressed girl with the name Athena on her badge bid her welcome and showed her to a table. 'Tea or coffee, Mrs Cole?'

Mrs Cole was already somewhat of a celebrity. At least in this dining room. 'Black coffee, please.'

The beverage was brought almost instantly, which was a contradiction, as the coffee was not instant but filtered, which Julie preferred.

'Please help yourself to the buffet breakfast, or if you prefer à la carte, please choose from the menu.'

'I will go for the buffet, thank you.'

Off to the corner of the room stood Mr Paniakos, who nodded when she approached the buffet and selected from the smorgasbord of delights before her.

Her plate filled quickly: fruit, small potato wedges, eggs, bacon, grilled halloumi cheese, hash browns, and some tomatoes. Toast was also available, and she quickly prepared two slices.

As she sat eating, she noticed several people dressed in business suits and office attire. *Maybe they're here for a conference*, she mused. She did not see anyone who looked like a reporter, so Mr Lakis must have been true to his word about keeping her visit secret. Perhaps that was why he chose this hotel, big enough to hide anyone in. Finishing her coffee and breakfast, she declined the offer of another cup before standing up.

Mr Paniakos was out of the blocks, walking swiftly towards her. 'I hope you enjoyed your breakfast. Is there anything you need? The car is on standby and waiting for you outside.'

'Thank you, but I'm going for a walk. All that food was a bit much, I need to get some exercise in now. I've got a map so I won't get lost.'

'As you wish, but please be careful. The place has been known to have pickpockets. Watch your belongings.'

'Thanks for the warning, Mr Paniakos, I shall do that.' She felt his words meant something else, like some implied threat to not go too far. Picking up her things, she nodded to Alexis, 'I don't need you today.'

'Please, Julie, wherever you are going, let me take you halfway. It is a long walk to the harbour.'

'I wasn't going there, but okay, if you want to take me. Maybe it will be good to ride a little way before I start exploring. As a tourist, you understand? I have never been to Paphos before, only the airport. So, thank you.'

6

MAX THE HAT

Julie opened her phone, selected contacts, and ran a finger all the way down to P; only Peter's old number was there. She returned to her messages, found Matthew's text, and shut the phone. The car spun away from the hotel and up the road.

'I will drop you by the big Church. It's a good landmark, so if you get lost ask for it. It's not far to walk to the harbour, or along the tourist road, up to the Tombs of the Kings. I can take you there too if you want to go.'

'No, the big Church is fine.' As they pulled up alongside the building, it was clear why it was called so.

'Its actual name is Agioi Anargyroi.' Alexis put on his tour guide hat.

'Big Church will do for me. I shall get a cab back so you go enjoy yourself. Go to the beach, meet some ladies, and I will see you tomorrow.'

He nodded and waved before driving the limo away.

Julie took out the map and walked in the direction the car had taken her the night before. She came to a corner pub, Ben's or Benjamin's the sign said, with just two or three customers seated at the bar. All looked local, no tourists she could see. She moved towards the bar.

A girl wearing a Guns N' Roses T-shirt that went well with her cool, wavy red hair approached her and said in a distinctly Londoner accent. 'What can I get you? beer, short, Frappé?'

'A Keo, please. Small one, thanks.'

The girl expertly snapped the top off the beer bottle with her lighter and placed it in front of Julie. 'Two Euros, thanks.'

She handed over a coin, which was quickly dropped into an open till, and the girl sank back behind the bar to read her magazine.

Looking around the room, she noticed a piano in the corner; nothing posh, but she assumed was still playable, as it looked in excellent condition. Seated next to the piano was a good-looking gent, possibly late fifties, and with a most distinctive look. He had almost sun-bleached white hair, with a ruddy complexion, and a pair of kind, dark-brown eyes. He smiled at her.

She returned the gesture and lifted the bottle at the same time as he did his. Whether he was the local gigolo, she wasn't sure, but he had a pleasant manner about him and as she sat down, he moved closer, introduced himself as Max the Hat, and plonked a Fedora hat on the table beside him. The other surprise was his fellow companion, a beautiful, extremely well-groomed and behaved Siberian Husky.

'Wolf cross. Bella, she is, in name and nature.' He sat stroking the dog's fur, proudly displaying her.

Julie pointed to the hat. 'Indiana Jones, eh?' Her American accent becoming pronounced on the word Indiana.

'Well, yes. Actually, it's a Herbert Johnson Poet Felt Fedora Hat, Light Sable Brown.'

'I bet you memorised that off the label so you can tell people you were Harrison Ford's double.' Julie picked up her bottle and sipped.

'I got it from someone who was, or at least he said he was. The hat and a jacket. Call it a souvenir.'

'Souvenir or theft, it suits you. I suppose you play the piano too?'

'Yes. Karaoke, DJ, singer, anything that keeps the plates spinning. Oh, and I write a little too.'

'A man of many talents. I am impressed, Mr Max the Hat. Can I get you a beer?'

'Allow me. Two Keos, Tracey, and Big Ones.'

'I can't drink one of those big bottles.'

'Drink what you like.'

Tracey snapped the tops off the two bottles and brought them across to the table.

Both raised their bottles. 'Cheers.'

'I'm sorry, I never introduced myself. Julie, Julie Cole.'

'I thought I recognised you. Your husband found the Aphrodite image and died last year. Is that why you are here, to pay homage to his memory?'

'Something like that.'

Max sensed he shouldn't pry. 'I don't know if I can help or even try, but if you ever need any assistance, I would be happy to lend a hand.'

Julie drank from the beer bottle again; it was going down quicker than she thought, and perhaps it was this that made her more relaxed. 'I would like to ask if you know where I can find this guy.' She took out a picture of Peter, the one she had taken at the Zygi Restaurant. It wasn't a great shot and he might have changed, but perhaps Max had seen him.

'This is who you're looking for?'

'Yes. Do you know him? His name is Peter Shaw, and he was Richard's best friend. He's in trouble and I need to find him.'

'Try Bar Street, some ex-pats go there. Which bar it will be, I don't know. A lot of them have closed, so it might be easier to track him down. That's your best bet. Sorry, I must go back to playing, was on my break.'

'But there's hardly anyone here to listen.'

'The idea is that when I play they come in. Good to meet you, Julie.' Max stood up and Bella shuffled with him back to the piano. 'What would you like to hear?'

'As time goes by.' Julie smiled and realised that she had in fact finished the large bottle of beer.

'You know, that's the first time anyone has asked for that?' He said with a smile.

Julie stood up, returned the smile, and turned to walk away. 'Play it Max.'

His fingers touched the keys, and his voice opened to the familiar refrain. 'You must remember this, a kiss is just a kiss, a sigh is just a sigh, the fundamental things apply, as time goes by…'

Julie left the bar, knowing she had made a new friend.

7

LIES LEAD TO MORE LIES

She was not more than fifty meters down the road when the sleek black limousine pulled up beside her. She stopped, tapped her foot twice, and waited for the window to roll down. 'Alexis, I told you I didn't need you. Go to the beach.'

'I can't, I have to be with you. It's orders from the office not to let you out of my sight. Where do you want to go now? I'll take you.'

'And I will have words with your bosses, I am supposed to be relaxing. Okay, take me to Bar Street. I don't know which bar or pub or club, so you sit in the car. You can watch me from a distance. If I need you I will shout.'

Alexis got the message.

Bar Street was once popular with the tourists. Tavernas, clubs, and pubs, especially after dark, did great business. There were a few problems with drugs, which the police always seemed to be in control of, and the obligatory drunk fights out in the square. But generally, it was a good place to go; there was even a bowling alley and a fish and chip shop close by.

Julie started her walk through the street, but all she could see were closed doors and shuttered windows. FOR SALE signs dotted the buildings from one side to the other; this was the recession in action. The soul of Bar Street was gone.

She went from one closed sign to the next until she reached a place with a few people in it. Most seemed oblivious to her and the surroundings, preferring to stare at the bottles and glasses littering the table, most of which were empty. She peered in the dingy doorway where perhaps five or six 'barflies' sat at the end of the room, and hoped Peter was among them. She dare not go in until she was sure. Taking out her phone, she searched for the number Matthew had given her. The phone rang three times before being picked up.

'Hello. Hello,' it was Peter.

She wanted to speak but couldn't. She hung up, then immediately dialled again.

'Hello,' this time the voice was agitated.

'Peter, it's Julie, don't hang up.'

'Julie…' Peter's voice quivered. 'Where are you?'

'If I have it right, I'm outside.'

Peter stood up and walked from the corner where he sat and out into the daylight.

His appearance shocked her. He was no longer the jovial spirit who had been so welcoming on her first visit. Instead, his clothes had outgrown him, his face looked unwashed, and his beard unkempt; he looked dirty and defeated. She walked across, grabbed him tight, held him in her arms, and tried to quell the tears in her eyes.

'How did you find me?' But he knew the answer before she could speak. 'Mathew. I told him to contact me if he needed anything and now, here you are. Why?'

'I needed to come to know the truth.'

'You know the truth. A hit-and-run killed Richard, that's it.'

'It's not, and you know it! For fuck's sake, Peter, tell me the truth, lies only lead to more lies. I need to know what really happened. You owe me that, as a friend, and Richard's friend.'

'I can't tell you, Julie, I don't know how.' There was genuine pain and angst on his face, as if he had been found out and was trying to backtrack. For a moment, he stood silent, just looking at her, wanting to speak but unable to. Instead, it was his turn to grab hold of her and clutch her to him tight as if he wanted to squeeze the truth into her so he would never have to give another answer. He let her go and smiled. Or tried to. 'Let me go pay what I owe. Then I'll come with you to talk.'

'I'm coming with you, not letting you out of my sight, Peter Shaw. Besides, before we do any talking you need a bath and shave. I'm staying at the Alexander the Great Hotel and that is where we are going now.'

'Fine, I could do with a clean-up.'

Julie went straight to the barman, asked for the bill, slipped a twenty Euro note over the counter, and left with Peter arm in arm.

The rest of the party in the corner paid no attention to his departure.

Alexis pulled up outside and the two got in.

Peter, mesmerized by drink and awe for this unexpected ride, made himself comfortable in the back seat, where Julie clung to his soiled shirt.

Keeping his eyes on the road, Alexis spun out of the road and into the main street; it wasn't long before they were at the Alexander, where the gates swung open to greet them.

Once again, Mr Paniakos greeted Julie, and her dishevelled passenger.

'Mr Shaw needs to freshen up. Can you also arrange for a time when he can see the barber and possibly the tailor? The bills are on me.' Julie felt a little like her namesake Julie Roberts in *Pretty Woman*, only this time, the roles were reversed.

Still unsure of what was happening and rather dazed by all the attention, Peter shuffled along as they made their way to the lift.

In suite number Four, Julie opened the bathroom door and pushed him inside. 'Get cleaned up, we have a lot to talk about.'

Peter stood looking into the three-sixty reflections. It was cruel to see the way he had deteriorated as a man. Once, those proud shoulders and acute blue eyes which could pick out an enemy sniper from a thousand feet were now bloodshot and filled with sadness. He had lost so much, and most he had no control over and his descent into loneliness had come swiftly.

He cleared the steam from the mirror, recalling the word TONIGHT Sheila had so cruelly written on the glass the night she set her plan in motion to kill Richard, and how thankful he was her actions had been thwarted.

He stripped, tearing off clothes from his sticky, smelly body, while the stench of beer on his breath permeated the room. He opened the door a fraction and pushed out the pile of filthy clothes.

He turned the shower on, the blasts from the jets a welcome invitation to climb in. The first hit him full force on his stomach, almost knocking him off his feet, but he revelled at the feel and softness of the water, as new spouts opened and the heat almost grilled him. Grime and dirt slipped from his body and a small patch of black gathered at his feet. He smiled, agog at being here, with Julie in the other room, waiting for some help. Maybe he was not as useless as he thought.

Still grinning, he lathered himself thoroughly, letting the foam spill across his body, contours, and down his neck. Such pleasure for such a minor act. Taking the shower head in his hand, he ran the water over his head, before adding shampoo and rubbing it into his scalp. The lather turned white and foamy as he rinsed off, making sure all suds had gone. He climbed out and wrapped himself with a fluffy white towel which just about fitted him then put on the complimentary bathrobe replenished by housekeeping after Julie's last escapade. He opened the door, letting some steam escape into the room. 'That is some shower.'

'I know,' she agreed. 'I got you some food, steak sandwich, French fries, and a salad.' Then she almost snapped at him. 'When was the last time you had a meal?'

He nodded and mumbled something, but his words were lost in the first bite, as he sat by the table and demolished the sandwich.

She watched him. Clearly, eating had not been one of his most urgent requirements.

'Thanks, this is great. When did you get here?' He continued to crunch and chat.

She sat impassively on the bed, waiting for him to finish. 'Yesterday. I got transferred here by a guy at the airport, said they wanted to look after me.'

'What else did *they* tell you?'

'Nothing, they told me nothing. Except to say how sorry they were to hear of Richard's demise. So, what do you know, and why are you in this state? I know you loved Richard, we all did, but you seem to have gone to pieces more than me. So, again, what do you know? I'm not stupid, Peter, no one just falls off the earth like you have, even if Sheila was a total bitch. You still have the kids and you still have us, but you cut them all out and went to a bottle. Why?'

A knock on the door interrupted.

Julie walked over, opened the door, and there stood the Key Porter, holding a small suitcase in his arms. He passed it to her. 'These are for your guest. We took the sizes from the discarded clothes you threw out.'

'Thank you.' She shut the door behind her and gave the suitcase to Peter. 'There's another room, go there to change, then we had better go see about that haircut and shave.'

The Key Porter watched as Peter scuttled into the next room, closing the door tightly behind him. 'Is there anything else, Mrs Cole?'

'No, thanks, we will be okay for now.' She sipped the

remainder of her black coffee as she waited for Peter to emerge. For a moment, she wondered if he might try to run, but they were four flights up and the only exit was through the main door. Her panic was obvious, she couldn't wait to question her friend.

Peter came out of the other room wearing a smart pair of black jeans, a red and white check shirt under a Pierre Cardin jumper, and on his feet he had black slip-on shoes. Apart from his unkempt beard, he looked quite reasonable. Attractive even.

'You like this look,' he said while standing to the left of Julie, pleased with his appearance.

'That is much better. Now, let's get your hair cut.'

'I owe you, Julie.'

'That's right, you do.'

8

THE HUNT BEGINS

*P*eter looked refreshed, and with the clean appearance and beard gone, he felt like a new man, even looking much younger.

Julie liked his fresh look too and taking him by the arm, almost frog-marched him out of the hotel. 'Right, you have had your shower, shave, and no doubt a shit too.'

Peter nodded, slightly embarrassed at the style of questioning.

'Now, I need… no, demand answers.'

'Yes, you do. And I will tell you what I know, but you won't believe it.'

Julie was becoming a little pissed off at his reluctance to divulge information.

'There is a restaurant across the road from here, English style, it's called Tea For Two. We will sit there, order a drink, and then I will tell you.'

They crossed the road and found a table in the restaurant's corner. Peter ordered tea and black coffee for Julie. The waitress, courteous and possibly foreign, was not interested in their conversation, merely bringing their order speedily and leaving them alone.

He made his tea; pouring the hot brown liquid from the small silver pot into the white china cup, then added milk slowly. All part of the delaying tactics he was trying to use to keep the hard questioning at bay. 'Julie, you must have an open mind about what I'm about to tell you.' His voice became a little shaky. 'Understand, there is more to this than most people would think possible, but I can tell you, it happened.'

'What, Peter?'

'The first thing to know is that Richard was not who he said he was… he was somebody else.'

'What? Who the fuck was he then, apart from the father of my children and my husband?'

'He was—'

'Perhaps you should allow me to explain to Mrs Cole, Mr Shaw. You know I am better suited.'

Julie's eyes lifted to follow the sombre voice, which came from a well-dressed Greek-looking gentleman. 'Excuse me, but who might you be, and how do you know my husband?'

Peter was about to speak, but before he could the Greek man presented himself.

'I am Lukas Christoulides. It is a pleasure to finally meet you, Mrs Cole.'

Julie sat back in her chair, she was not expecting this.

'I understand you wish to get some answers about Richard… and his other personality. Please allow me to entertain you tonight and we will explain everything then. I will send for you around 7:30 pm, and Mr Shaw, of course. Until tonight, I wish you a pleasant afternoon.'

As quickly and as mysteriously as he arrived, he departed, followed by a small group of cohorts.

'What the fuck… What was all that about?' Pure Bostonian rang from her mouth.

'I agree, let him explain. It's so much better coming from him.' Peter took his escape ticket and poured himself another cup of tea.

'You know something, tell me.'

'I truly can't, Julie, so let Lukas do it. Just wait until tonight, you will know it all then.'

DRACOS HAD HIS ORDERS; track down the Gorgon's head and return it to Hades, which he himself had been trying to do for some time, but the hunt had gone cold. Somehow, someone had removed it from where it had always been and he needed to find it before anyone else did. Hades had not been altogether explicit why he required it, but either way no one was taking any chances.

The power of resurrection could potentially upset the Underworld's balance and in the wrong hands cause chaos; all kinds of spirits might suddenly be reawakened, and that would not do. In the Underworld, there must always be balance. Hades was convinced his all-powerful brother, Zeus, was behind the mystery, but it could just as well be one of his other siblings, or one of the offspring. Because, who could forget Aphrodite's adventure into monster-unleashing the previous year. What he did know was that rumours led to trouble. The question was, why would any of them want the blood, and what were they planning to do with it?

That had now become Dracos' business; to figure out who was behind it and get answers to the questions that were bubbling up by the minute. Such as, why was the wife of a certain dead mortal in Cyprus? Why was she at the location of his demise? And, what did she have to do with anything? But the oracle had been quite clear concerning that, 'watch for the dead man's wife, she bears more harm to you than any other'. If that was the case, he had no problem handling her too.

The seat on the Easy Jet flight to Paphos was too small for Dracos' bulk, and his small carry-on bag raised a few suspicions. Security expected a large man to have large luggage and as it was the only thing he carried, they wanted a look inside. It contained a book and two small wooden figurines depicting a stag and an eagle made of wood, only three inches long. Patiently, he explained that they belonged to his Mother; old family heirlooms. This seemed to satisfy the man's curiosity to allow them on board.

He tried to sleep but the passenger beside him kept shifting positions, probably to get away from his hulking size, the agitation continuing until Dracos got up and went the restroom. While he washed his face, the flight became bumpier and the seatbelt light flashed on. As a storm started, lightning crashed around the plane and it shifted altitude to escape the tempest. Navigating an unstable aisle, he noticed a lot of frightened faces on his way back to his seat and heard a few muffled screams as another bolt of lightning boomed close to the fuselage. Not quite the welcome he was expecting. Was his visit already known in some quarters, or was it coincidence? The storm subsided and the plane resumed its course.

He did not hurry or draw attention to himself as he disembarked, although he felt several pairs of eyes watching him. He lined up with the other tourists and passed through immigration, noticing the collage of pictures of Aphrodite's Rocks on the walls.

Out in the entrance hall, he made for the taxi rank, where several cars waited. He handed one driver a piece of paper and pointed. 'Take me there.'

The driver skimmed it as Dracos got in the car.

There were no other words exchanged until the car pulled up outside a large villa close to the village of Mandria, only five or six miles from the airport and ten from Paphos. Dracos climbed out of the cab, took the key from his pocket, and closed the door behind him as the taxi drove away.

~

AFTER AGREEING to meet Julie again in the lobby at 7:00 pm, Peter went home to change. They would have a drink in the bar before their meeting with Mr Christoulides.

Unsure of what to wear, Julie opted for a conservative dress, lime green with white trim, black shoes, and her beloved rose charm necklace. It had been Richard's favourite.

Carrying the folded notes in her handbag, she closed the suite's door and made her way down the hall to the lift. She climbed in, pressed the button, and almost at once a strange vapour entered the lift, as if someone were smoking. Yet, there was no smell of smoke.

But with the mist came the voice from her dreams. 'He is not dead. He is not dead.'

The lift stopped, she stepped out, and the vapour faded. A little shaken by the experience, she dashed towards Peter. 'I'm ready for that drink.'

He had done his best to make himself look presentable, and the shave had certainly done the trick, by bringing out his famous rosy cheeks back into bloom.

Julie took him by the arm and they made their way to the bar. 'What will you have, Peter? And no, not a beer. Pick something more exotic. After all, we are on an island.' She said, smiling and feeling relaxed again.

'In that case, I will have a Mai Tai.'

'Excellent choice, and I will have a Manhattan.'

The head barman, an expert cocktail waiter, leapt into action, picking up bottles, spinning them in the air, and throwing ice into the glasses, whirling on two feet and catching another batch of cubes before crushing them. A perfectly performed little routine. He placed the two drinks side by side sporting swizzle sticks and straws. 'Enjoy.'

Julie clinked her glass against Peter's. The show was over and there would be no time for another. 'Cheers. It's so good to see you, especially when looking like your old self again.'

Peter smiled and exchanged pleasantries, but his guilt overwhelmed him, because she deserved a decent explanation. An approaching figure saved him the trouble.

Mr Paniakos said. 'Excuse the interruption, your car is waiting outside.'

Julie checked her watch, almost seven thirty. She downed what was left of the Manhattan, leaving a cold tingle on her lips. 'Thank you.'

Peter followed her to the waiting Limousine.

9

———————————

WHAT IS TRUTH?

*A*lexis was smartly dressed in a black suit, white shirt, and bow tie. He ushered Julie in first, then Peter, shut the door, and climbed in behind the wheel. 'Please buckle up, we have some way to travel. I have called ahead and told them we will be a little late. Do not worry, I will get us there as quickly as possible.' He was true to his word, hitting the accelerator hard.

As soon as he was through the small town streets and out onto the open road, the lights became sparse by comparison to the street lights of Paphos. As they began to climb the mountain road, they could see the harbour lights and what looked like search beams streaming upwards from the Fort.

Full headlights on, the vehicle chased around the sharp winding roads as it sped on and up. From her window, Julie saw signs for Laatchi and Aphrodite's Bath flashing by. Even now, the goddess was still everywhere.

About thirty-five kilometres from town, Alexis began to slow down and turned into a narrow dirt lane, the ride becoming bumpier with each bend. Thankfully, the car had good suspension. Ahead of them two rows of lit torches appeared, leading to a longer line and an even sharper curve. The limo slid around the corner, its wheels gripping the new dirt road. Alexis slowed down.

A man holding a flaming torch in one hand and dressed in a monk's black cassock approached the car and pointed down the road. Ahead and surrounded by dense bushes, was a huge white gate and behind it, a magnificent villa, bedecked in ancient sculptures and figures.

Julie peered through the window as the car came to a halt then stepped out onto the marble floor as soon as Alexis opened the door. Peter followed. Alexis climbed back in, started the car again, and spun the wheels to return to where he had just driven from.

Julie marvelled at the magnificence of her surroundings.

At the door stood Mr. Lukas. 'Please, this way.'

Julie obliged obediently. Peter not two steps behind her.

'Welcome, come in.' Lukas led the way through corridors festooned with Greek art and sculptures, its magnificence comparable to a fine arts museum.

Both entered the dining area where a table lay spread with an array of food that could adorn any king's palace.

Two men stood up to greet the guests. One was Mr Lakis from the airport, the other, Julie had not seen before, but Peter thought he had.

Lukas offered his guests two chairs, while two young ladies dressed in old style Grecian dresses, passed them into their seats.

Lukas broke the silence. 'You met Mr Lakis at the airport.'

Julie nodded and Lakis smiled in return.

'This gentleman is Theodorous.'

The elder man stood, then sat back down.

'Now that the formalities are over, no doubt you are filled with questions. But first, allow me to soften your palate with this rather lovely drink.' Lukas began to pour the slow flowing liquid into two glasses. It was like watching treacle. 'Drink, it is delicious, tastes a little like honey.'

Julie picked up the glass, took two sips, and nodded, Lukas was right. She smiled, while noticing how rich his accent was, his English so much better than when he first met Richard. She recalled Richard telling her that he spoke English, but not well. Apparently, he had been taking lessons.

'You like the drink? It is called Ambrosia, or nectar of the gods.'

Julie stopped and looked at him. His eyes had become brighter and his figure had grown larger.

He took a deep breath before saying. 'And you, Julie Cole, are in the presence of gods. Mr Shaw already knows this to be true.'

Clearly, the Ambrosia's real objective was kicking in because she did not recall having been introduced to the three men who now sat before her. Yet, they still resembled Lukas, Lakis, and Theodorous.

'My name is not Lukas Christoulides, my brothers and sisters call me Zeus. This is Aeolus, he controls the winds and tempests. And the other is my brother-in-arms, Poseidon. So, Mrs Cole, today you are in the presence of the Gods of Olympus. Let it not frighten you, but I thought this was the best way to explain the connection between your husband and my daughter Aphrodite.'

Julie stared at them, barely managing to keep her mouth closed. 'I don't know what is in that drink, but it has messed with my head and I don't believe a word you're saying. This is some masquerade party... Someone is going to come from behind that curtain with a fucking camera and ask me to smile. All I want is the truth, to know who or what killed my husband.'

Peter tried to calm her down.

She shrugged him off. 'Are you in on this too? I thought you were our friend. What the hell have you done to me, Peter? what is going on here?'

'Please, Mrs Cole, calm down and I will tell you what you

want to know. But from your reaction I can see already it will be difficult for you to understand.'

Anger dripped from her words. 'TRY ME.' The rich Bostonian twang had returned.

Lukas walked away from the table. 'You ask for the truth? Truth, Mrs Cole, is subjective. Or even a lie, when we try to settle an argument or an injustice we cannot comprehend. The only time you ever really know the truth is when it is in front of you. Indisputable, not hearsay, not what people tell you, because truth is not always real, merely a method to hide facts, because facts are the only real truth we ever have.'

Julie tried to understand what he was saying but couldn't grasp it, she needed something more.

'It is a fact that I am Zeus, King of the Gods. It is also a fact that I am standing before you. This is one fact you cannot ignore. The other facts are that my companions are also gods of Olympus. Aeolus and Poseidon stand before you too, another fact. Whether you believe what I say is true or not, is for you to decide. But truth can only be confirmed by fact. Do you understand that what your eyes see and your ears hear, is fact? that it is undisputable?'

'Fine, Mr Lukas, Zeus, or whatever you want to be called, but it doesn't explain the fact, as you put it, why you are here. These are myths, legends, written down in books by Homer, Aristotle, Sophocles, and those other philosophers of ancient times. And what about the Iliad and all the trials of Hercules? Oh, and Jason and the Golden Fleece. Pure mythology. Fairy tales for adults.'

'Not so, Mrs Cole. Hercules is real, his actual name, as we call him, not the Romans, is Heracles and he works as a mechanic in Paphos. But that is by the by.'

'See? now you're just taking the piss out of me. Hercules or Heracles, whatever his goddamn name is, a mechanic… this is some kind of set-up to put me off. Look, Zeus, or whatever, I don't mean to be rude but how can you be here when you don't exist? And if you did thousands of years ago, how and why are you still here?'

'Oh, Mrs Cole… may I call you Julie?'

She nodded.

'I wish it was that simple to explain. The best thing to say is that we never left. We have always been here—because we are immortal—just in different guises. You see all these statues of me, Poseidon, and Aphrodite? What do you suppose they were based upon? They were taken from real life, sculpted in our image at first, then changed over the years, adaptations of us. We too adapted, had to, as mankind and the mortal world became ever less reliant on the old gods. New religions gained focus and we went into hiding, if you like. We were not needed anymore. Yes, the Romans changed our names and made us their gods, but by then we were old ways, and may I say, reclusive. Preferring to watch from a distance, never interfering, and never getting involved with any mortal issue. We simply moulded ourselves into whatever society we needed to be with. Is this a little clearer?'

Is it possible? She had always relied on rational thought, but this… it was incomprehensible. Yet, here they stood before her, large as life.

'Let us take a break, some food and wine, and perhaps some music. Let us relax, it is much to think about and I can see you are having a hard time understanding what I told you. But those are the facts. Please come to the table and sit. Have some of this delicious food.'

'Fine, thank you, but before I do that, I want you to answer one question.'

'Please, go ahead. I may not know the answer but ask.'

'Was my husband killed in a road accident?'

'No, he was not.' Zeus looked straight at her and then towards Peter.

'Your husband is not dead.' A female voice said.

Julie recognised it instantly. It was the one from her dreams, her nightmares, the one that had haunted her all this time, and now, here she stood. Her nemesis.

Zeus turned to his brother. 'I told you, Poseidon, to never let her out, she is not wanted here.'

Aphrodite strolled into the assembled company, her nonchalance a trademark of her beauty. 'It's nice to see you again, Father.'

'She said she had an important message for Mrs Cole and that it could only be delivered in person.' Poseidon said, embarrassed, then continued somewhat remorseful. 'Told me a sliver of it and it sounded like we should pay attention, so that's why she is out of her cage. Still, I apologise.'

Julie stood, stunned by the new arrival. She wanted, no, demanded more information. 'What do you mean he's not dead? Peter?' She turned to him for reassurance.

He sat still, either unable or unwilling to comment.

Aphrodite sauntered closer to Julie. She too was dressed in the classical Grecian dress, with a braid of hair wrapped like a laurel crown over her forehead. Her eyes twinkled and sparkled, a radiance that all the time in confinement could not contain. She picked up a small bunch of grapes and began to nibble at the fruit. 'Your husband is not dead, but he is under Hades' protection in the Underworld. If we don't act quickly, we will lose him forever.'

'How do you know this?' Zeus pressed.

'I speak to Persephone when she is let out from the Underworld for six months of the year.' She turned to Julie. 'She is Hades' wife, but hates him, and will never forgive him for snatching her and taking her by force. So now, she does anything she can to hurt him, which is why she is willing to help us. She told me the cycle will be complete by the next full moon and then Richard's soul will be his. If we don't act fast, he will be gone.'

Julie was taken aback. 'Wait a minute, young lady. You may be offering some kind of help, but who said you have anything to do with this?'

'I do because I am responsible. I brought Richard to the island, believing him to be someone else, and I was right.'

'Who?'

'Adonis, my lover. In the end, Richard was Adonis, but I was too late to save him. Not even my all-powerful Father could save either of them because by then, they were two souls wrapped in one body.'

Julie plopped onto a chair, shock inadequate to describe her thoughts. Peter stood beside her while the room fell silent. Gods and mortals gathered together, unable to speak for a moment.

'What my Daughter tells you is right.' Zeus said. 'Richard and Adonis were one and the same. Aphrodite knew this the day Richard asked her to bring him home safely from the war; it was something Adonis always did whenever he went into battle or on a hunt. But you interrupted her mission, and she wanted revenge, not just on you but on Richard too. Her elaborate plan to use a creature from the darkness was the only way she knew Richard would return. Mayhem and chaos across the island created that opportunity, and of course he fell into her trap, by simply wanting to stop the senseless deaths. Still, she was not certain, until the fatal moment when he lay dying on the beach. Before he passed, he spoke in ancient Greek and she saw his face change to Adonis. As his blood flowed, a field of anemones clustered around him. But by then both souls had passed into the Underworld.'

'So, who did I bury?' Julie was more than a little confused and perplexed.

'You did not look inside the casket, correct? You were told not to, as the injuries were severe.'

'Yes, they said to remember him as he was, not to see him as a corpse.'

'He was flown home in a sealed coffin filled with stones, because the two bodies were already on their way to the Underworld. The arrangements were made by my office.'

'None of this makes any sense. See it from my point of view,' Julie tried to get a grip on what she was being told. 'First, you are not Mr Christoulides, but Zeus, "King of the Gods", and all these people around you are gods as well. Then, my husband who is not really my husband but a demigod, is not dead but inside the body of Adonis who is Aphrodite's lover. Who is not dead either and both have been sent to the Underworld. Now, we have a little time in which to rescue them. Oh, and the body I buried who was supposed to be my husband is not my husband but a pile of rocks...' Her sarcasm was tangible. 'How am I doing so far? And one other thing, most of you must be over five thousand years old, so how the fuck are you still alive?'

'I told you it would be hard to understand.' Zeus said and stroked his chin.

'It's a pile of horse shit,' her accent was deep. 'As for you, young lady, you had me believing you were floating in the water, but then I knew you were just my imagination gone wild. Aphrodite, or whatever your name is, what I saw in the waters was just an apparition. Not real. In fact, I think you are all actors and this is some ruse to get me off the island.' Her temper boiled over.

Zeus rose from his seat and said. 'I told you the facts and I only deal in those. So, Mrs Cole, as you still doubt my words and that of my brothers and Daughter, let me show you once and for all who we really are.'

Aphrodite grabbed her Father's arm. 'Are you sure?' There was genuine concern on her face.

'Proof does not matter.' Aeolus remonstrated with Zeus. 'So what if she doesn't believe? you don't have to do this.'

'It is the only way. Now, believe!'

The figures in front of the two mortals began to metamorphose into their true selves.

Zeus threw off his mortal shell and transformed into his omnipotent self; his stature rising from the floor to tower above the cowering humans. The ceiling opened to display the night sky, even as Zeus' figure grew taller with every second, his body magnificent and lean, his neck and shoulders perfectly formed, as if he had been sculpted. His face, beaming down on the two shaking humans, allowed itself a sly grin as his bright green eyes lit up his expression. The silver locks of his mane shone in the moonlight. His imposing figure turned majestically towards his fellow Olympians who likewise had adopted their godly personas.

Poseidon stood next to Zeus, his brother. He had lost the fragility of old age and in its place stood a giant of a man, festooned in a netting green skirt. His bare chest glistened with beads of water that ran from his torso like rivulets and in his hand he brandished a golden trident. He held the weapon high above his head, thrusting it towards the night sky while holding a large net which curled tightly around his fingers. Beneath him, small pools of sea water fermented on the floor.

To his right stood the impressive and equally imposing figure of Aeolus, whose grip on the bag that held the four winds was as strong as the tempest trying to escape his grasp. All three gods stood resolute in front of the mortals.

Not to be left out from this trio of deities, Aphrodite disposed of the comfort of her mortality to stand with her Father. As if this display was not enough to convince anyone in the room of the truth of their existence.

Zeus, his beard white and hanging beyond his collar, stepped forward, leaned down to a fold in his robe, and pulled out a shaft of brilliant light which he extended until it was at least six feet long. Holding it firmly in his right hand, he stretched out his arm and flexed his taught muscles. In a Moses-like gesture, he slammed the lightning bolt down onto the marble floor. A chunk shattered and small chips flew through the air. As tiled shrapnel tore across the room, Zeus struck again, but this time, the whole room lit up. Flashes of lightening whizzed from one side to the other, followed by a massive clap of thunder that made the floor and walls shake, rendering the cherished statues into worthless rubble, as they began to topple over.

Not content, Zeus orchestrated more lightning displays so they became a strobe light. Everything went into suspended animation as the figures moved in slow motion and the lightning bolts intensified.

Julie covered her eyes and crouched on the floor, the crackle of thunder bolts and the bristling of electricity skirting over her body, while Peter held her tight. The cracking of the last bolt so much louder than all the others and the flash so intense it had to have been heard and lit up the place for miles. It all stopped. Shaking and in tears, she clung to Peter, her voice repeating softly. 'I'm sorry, I'm sorry.' Then she admitted, unless she were drugged, the facts were before her. She was in the presence of gods, and if so, then all they said had occurred between Richard and Aphrodite must also be real. There were no disparaging remarks or sarcasms, just blind faith in whatever was happening. Gratefully, she accepted Peter's hand as he helped her up from the floor.

Lukas was the first to speak. 'I suggest you stay here tonight. Don't worry, the car will collect you in the morning. So, from the information we have, we know we need to move quickly, plan something if we are to rescue your husband.' He cast an eye towards his daughter. 'You must work with Aphrodite, no matter how upsetting that may be. We will also need to open secrets that have long been forgotten in order for your Odyssey to begin. But we will discuss our strategy after we have eaten. I think we are all in need of refreshment now.'

Still shaking, Julie nodded in agreement and along with Peter joined the gods at the table as food began to be served. Gradually, acceptance resonated throughout the room, the overall atmosphere that of calm after the storm and with it the most surreal setting possible, mortals and immortals eating and drinking together, in silence.

Lukas reverted to his usual form even as his phone began to ring. 'Excuse me, I must take this.' He moved to the far end of the room, away from earshot, and muttered. 'Tell me... yes... When did he arrive? Is he being watched? Why not? Do that, now... No, I don't want the boy used for that... send one of the others... What else? The Temple, you say... Sure Hades is behind this? Find out all you can. If he seeks the Gorgon's Head, he means to stop us. No... I said no. We have less time than I thought and with Hades involved there will be even less. Yes, do that. Thank you.' A deep frown furrowed his semblance and gave him a worrying look as he returned to the table. 'We need to move sooner than I thought. Aphrodite, you must prepare Julie, and, Mr Shaw, you will go with them. After dinner, we will discuss our next move. I am disturbed by what I just heard, as this could upset the balance between our worlds. I cannot afford to let that happen.' He sat back down but did not touch his food again. Instead, he poured another glass of Ambrosia and drank slowly.

~

DRACOS HAD ALREADY RECEIVED notification from Hades about what he needed to do next and when, so he sat in the villa's kitchen drinking Greek coffee; he liked it rich and thick. After taking the last sip, he got up, moved over to the cupboard, and pressed a small red button next to the fridge.

A concealed wall opened. He stepped inside, switched on the light, and selected weapons from the stacked arsenal. He chose two handguns and an Uzi; he liked the weight and feel of the weapon. As a special ops soldier, he had used the weapon in various operations during the Balkans conflict, but for close combat, he always used his scimitar.

Becoming a mercenary after the war was second nature, as he operated across all areas: Angola, Iraq, Afghanistan, and it was whilst on a mission and passing through Greece that he met Hades, who soon introduced him to the pleasures of his world. It wasn't long before he became a member of the Temple of Necromanteion, a place where he could fulfil his own darkest desires. Hades bid his time before telling him who he really was, making certain this was the right man. Dracos never flinched; he had seen too much and had more blood on his hands than he cared about, so to become a servant to the master of Death was a promotion. Now ensconced in Hades' way of thinking and operating, he simply obeyed.

He walked out from the armoury and back into the kitchen, placed the bag he had brought with on the table, opened it, and took out the two wooden figurines. Reaching into a kitchen drawer, he grabbed a sharp knife and a pair of pliers and cut inside the handle. Peeling back the plastic, he took out a long thin strand of piano wire. Deftly handling the razor-sharp edge, he poked it through the hole in the first figure, twisting it with the pliers. He repeated the process with the other figure then gave a slight tug between the two; the perfect tool for silent executions.

Placing the killing tool on the table, he opened his phone and clicked through the picture files. Usually, he took pictures with a camera then transferred them to his phone, and from time to time he looked at them. This was one of his favourite and special things he enjoyed doing, and as he browsed the gallery, the memories came flooding back.

The first set of pictures was of a group of young men, the eldest probably twenty, whom he had despatched with an Uzi.

The rest of the executed bodies lay crumpled across the dirt road, before being pushed into a ditch. This had taken place the day before the main massacre in Srebrenica in July 1995. He had been part of a covert-ops team, which came across this group trying to escape. But once captured, there was none. He and his buddies saw to that.

The Bosnian War had been the best training ground for the young Dracos; as it was where he perfected his killing abilities, knowing full well that he would get away with it. His excursion to Angola was not as straightforward as his enemies were, just as merciless, and he often wondered if the mission was worth the fee. He spent long hours in the bush, avoiding snakes, wild animals, and the guerrillas.

The next batch of pictures showed the bodies of the 'child soldiers' he had dispatched. They had been in a group marching through the bush, their heads barely visible against the tall grass. Dracos, heavily camouflaged, took his position and as the kids moved forward, opened up with his sniper rifle, picking off one by one in rapid fire. All fell like ducks off a fun fair shelf, biting the dirt as they dropped. When the shooting stopped and only the bush sounds could be heard, Dracos stood over them and with camera in hand began shooting, this time with his camera, before riddling the children with bullets from his Uzi. In some pictures, Dracos' shots were so perfect that their faces were totally blown away.

As he moved from image to image, each becoming more obscene than the last, he felt his manhood throb. These pictures always did the trick. Moving his hand down to his zipper, he pulled it down, then released the top button on his jeans, before plunging his hand inside.

10

PERFECT THOUGHT

*I*f what had transpired already was not bewildering enough, the next few hours became even more so. It was hard enough to grasp that they were in the presence of gods, and to be given a glimpse of their world was difficult to comprehend, or come to terms with, but to sit with them and make plans was beyond unreal.

Lukas convened with his daughter and the other two gods as they poured over a book he had taken from the table, which was written in ancient Greek, although there were some accompanying illustrations. 'Julie,' he spoke. 'I know you love Richard deeply and would do anything you could to get him back.'

'I would.' Julie's voice was quiet but assured.

'Then look at me when I query this, for you must truly understand what I ask. Because this is not something you can enter into without *perfect thought*.'

'I don't understand… *perfect thought?*'

'*Perfect thought* means you have considered every aspect of the situation; your children, way of life, everything you live by, and decide there is only one course of action.'

'Yes, I have decided.' She felt confused but knew he was going to ask something else.

'But do you really understand what I mean about *perfect thought*? Or what is at stake? Your life, your children's lives, your very soul. Are all worth that risk? Because you will face things that your imagination can't even create. You are going into what you would call Hell. There is no easier way to say it.' Lukas emphasized the point, perhaps a little too well.

'If it means I can get Richard back, yes, I am ready to walk into Hell.' Julie wore her *don't fuck with me,* expression.

Lukas could sense her passion and strength, but above all, her courage.

Aphrodite spoke. 'Good, because I don't want a coward walking into that place with me.'

The animosity between them returned with one sentence.

'Enough, Daughter, you know the only way is to work together. Now, let us work out a strategy because I learnt today that we are not the only ones involved. Hades has sent one of his servants and I suspect he's on the same plan as you to capture the Gorgon's blood, or her head. The Temple has always wanted it, for it would give Hades and the Underworld greater power.'

Julie looked confused.

As did Peter, who leaned across the table, his question aimed at Lukas. 'What exactly is Gorgon's blood and why do we need it, or why does this other crowd want it?'

'A brief lesson, Mr Shaw, because history books are the maps of time. When you read them you embark on a journey, an odyssey if you like, as did Perseus when he slew Medusa on his own Odyssey, after which, he carried the Gorgon's head away and used it against the Kraken.'

'Well, that's what happened in the film.'

Lukas laughed. 'You mortals… a film. Don't you ever read books? No matter. The Gorgon's blood is Medusa's, and it still flows within her hair in the serpents she has on her head. Her magic is all-powerful, even in death hence why Hades has long desired it. He imagines it will bring him and the Temple overwhelming power over the realm of the dead.'

'Wouldn't it?' Peter said.

Lukas shrugged. 'It does not matter what he believes, we will not let him achieve it.'

'You keep mentioning a Temple. Which one is that?' Julie piped up.

Lukas looked at her. 'The Temple of Necromanteion, Hades and his wife, Persephone, rule it. When bodies decay upon the earth, their souls are released, and they travel through the fissures in the soil to the Underworld. These spirits possess abilities that the mortal world does not, becoming like Oracles able to predict the future. Hades has built shrines close to the entrances of the Underworld, where the dead meet to perform their necromancy rituals to give and receive prophecies.'

'Interesting,' Julie said, 'but what does all that have to do with us?'

'One such prophecy foretold of your coming.'

'This is getting heavy.' Julie's expression of angst was not lost on Peter.

Aphrodite remained aloof as she stood listening and waiting for her moment.

'Before you continue,' Julie said. 'May I ask why it's necessary for me to go to the Underworld? You are all gods, proved it to me, so why can't you click your fingers or bang that silver thing in your pocket and voilà, Richard is back with us?'

'I wish it was that simple, but it's not possible. As Zeus, I cannot enter the Underworld, because if I did, Hades would imprison me and the balance of the gods would be gone. You asked earlier how we have survived, not just as immortals, but how we continued living amongst you? The simple answer is that we had to adapt. We never crossed over into the old ways, going with the times. Hades is the only god able to move between his world and this one because he controls death. Which brings us to a potential problem, the only proper way to reach the other side is to die; we hope this will not happen to you. Which is why we need you to understand *perfect thought*. But even if perchance you succeed, the price may still be too high. You may release Richard, but there may be a penalty to pay, where your soul is the offering.'

'I love my husband.' Julie's answer asserted her commitment.

Lukas took her by the hand. 'I see why Richard chose you.'

Aphrodite's wry smile was meant to intimidate, but Julie was long past that. Adrenaline rushed in her veins, whatever she had to do, whatever the sacrifice, she was ready.

'We agree then that we must start as soon as possible. Now, let us explain the first part of this journey. You and Mr Shaw will travel to Crete, to Mount Dicte. It is my birthplace and where I keep my most precious treasures, the Golden Fleece, the Arrow that killed Achilles, and the Gorgon's head. The blood has two powers; one is to kill by poisoning, and the other is to resurrect. She also wears a mask which is what the Greeks call apotropaic; its meaning is to ward off evil. By wearing the mask, we hope evil spirits will not enter the Gorgon's head and use her power. This is also why she is enclosed in a box of mirrors, so that should her eyes open again, she will only reflect her own image and no one else's.'

'You seem to have thought of everything.'

'You would think so.' Lukas smiled. 'But this is just the beginning. Once at Mount Dicte, you need to find the entrance to my sanctuary, the Dikteon Cave. It splits into five chambers; there is an upper and lower section. The top cave is like a rocky cavern, but to go where you need to be, you must travel down some steep steps to the lower cave called Kato Spileo. What you are looking for is the lake at the bottom. The entrance is under-water, but not deep. Above the lake are hanging rocks and in the centre of those is the *Mantle of Zeus*, something that resembles a chandelier.

'You need to go directly under this rock and swim to the bottom where there is a small inlet that leads to my cave. Nobody knows this, but it's where I was born, hidden by my Mother to protect me from my Father Cronus. Who would have eaten me if he had the chance as he did some of my other siblings. His jealousy was so potent, he could not bear the thought of one of his heirs ruling. But that is another story.' There was passion in Lukas' eyes, as if those memories stirred real rage. 'You will need to do this at night, as many people visit the caves during the day.

'Within the cave, you will see all my treasures. The Gorgon's head is kept under the stone table. Be careful when you raise the box and the lid, you seek the serpent whose colouring is purple. Take a knife from the table, cut into the flesh, and gather the blood into this cup.' He leaned across and presented Julie with a silver chalice. 'Once the blood is inside, the chalice will seal itself, and it will remain shut until you find Richard. Then you must drip the blood into his mouth. This will be how you resurrect him. Do you understand?

'Mr Shaw, although both of you need to do this, only Julie can enter the Underworld. You must remain outside. Aphrodite will join you there, she will not be with you until then. In Crete, my messenger Hermes, who has the illustrious title of *Guide of Souls* will meet with you and take you to Mount Dicte.' He moved closer to Julie. 'Now, listen carefully. As I mentioned before, you will not be the only one in this endeavour. Hades seeks the Gorgon's head, not just the blood, so his messenger is already here on the island. He is mortal, but also a ruthless killer, so we are watching him. You must be careful because he will surely try to kill you both.'

'Lukas, I'm a humble woman, who knows nothing about killing. Yes, I am an army wife but I have only ever shot a rifle once, and that was when I was twelve. How am I expected to stop a killer?'

'Mr Shaw has experience of war, and he also took on the Scylla. He will protect you.'

Peter smiled nervously. 'Thank you for your confidence, but I'm sorry, I don't have the skills for this job. Up against a natural killer? Sure, I shot at the Scylla with a shotgun, but if what you say is true, I am out of my depth here. Surely you have some warrior-god you can send instead and protect both of us. How about Heracles? You said he's in Paphos, working as a mechanic. He probably could do this job.' Peter shivered with genuine fear, and perhaps the lack of alcohol.

Zeus stood up and walked around the room, not once, but twice. Deep in thought, he whispered, looking straight at the two mortals. 'It is not possible to send anyone else who is immortal. Only Aphrodite will be with you, and only when you enter the Underworld. Her deity is bound by mortal belief. If you cannot do this, then Richard is lost, as I cannot help you. You must choose. So, it is *perfect thought* or go back to England.'

Julie got to her feet. 'No, I am not returning without my husband. If this is what I need to do, then I will. I just need some weapon or some protection.'

Lukas placed his hands around the back of his head and plucked a medallion from under his shirt.

Julie stared at it. She had seen the symbol many times before in tourist shops around the island.

'Wear this, it will ward off the evil eye and protect you.'

Taking the medallion from him, she placed the brilliantine blue eye which captured the light perfectly around her neck, and immediately felt warm safety cocooning her.

'We must get ready, for your odyssey begins soon and arrangements have been made. You will fly to Crete tomorrow.'

Julie thanked Lukas. 'When will Aphrodite meet us?'

Lukas held her hand. 'Once you have the Gorgon's blood and

the next part of your journey begins. Hermes will guide you through that stage. For now, both of you have enough to concentrate on. It's late and dawn will soon be upon us, so go, your beds are prepared. Mr Shaw, there are two women waiting to serve you.'

'Thank you, but tonight I just need to sleep. This has been a very long day.'

'Yes, it has.' Lukas moved away from the couple, took the hand of one of the hostesses, and they walked together to his bedroom.

11

THE ODYSSEY BEGINS

*A*lexis drove the vehicle slowly down the pathway. In daylight, he could see just how narrow the road was and how close he was to the edge of the hill. He waved at the one guard who stood on duty about a hundred feet from the entrance to the villa and the gates swung open. He drove in, parked, and waited.

Julie emerged first, followed by Peter, while Lukas stood by the door, having said all their goodbyes and felicitations inside.

'All set?' Alexis asked as he started the car and looked across to Julie, while smiling the smile of youth. He never questioned what he was asked to do, he just got on with it.

'Alex, we must go back to the hotel. I have to pack and Mr Shaw needs to be dropped off at home, he needs his stuff.'

'No need, all done. Everything is in the cases in the boot, all your clothes and travel documents. Mr Shaw's are there too.'

Peter spoke from the back of the car. 'Why am I not surprised?'

She turned around, sensing his apprehension, and could almost hear his silent question, 'What the hell am I doing here and how did I get involved in this?'

The car spun down the driveway, onto the path, and made its way towards the main road. Once there, it moved swiftly through traffic, speeding up past one car, sometimes two. As soon as Alexis saw the road was clear ahead, he smiled and pushed the throttle down. 'I hope you had a pleasant evening, Julie.'

'It was enlightening. Very interesting.' She had no idea how much he knew about their hosts.

'The private jet has been chartered and it will have just the two of you as passengers. You leave in about an hour. I believe Mr Lakis arranged it.'

'A private jet, I have never flown in one of those before.' Julie smiled.

Peter chipped in. 'I think this is going to be the first time for a lot of things in this odyssey of yours.'

She nodded. Perhaps she was beginning to understand just what was being asked of her and what *perfect thought* really was.

DRACOS KEPT in the slipstream of Alexis' car. He had followed the vehicle from Paphos and pulled off into a side road, where he had taken out his binoculars and watched as it drove slowly down the slope to the villa. Aware of the guards around the property, he kept a safe distance. But once they left, he could drop back behind them into traffic as they made their descent down the hill.

The boy drove faster than usual, bobbing in and out between cars as he accelerated past them in the slow lane, before switching back into the single lane, so that must mean they were going somewhere.

In the speeding vehicle, Alexis checked his watch, making sure he was on time, while Julie and Peter sat in the back, their fingers gripping the leather seats. He swung the car onto the main highway just as the Paphos airport sign loomed large in front of them and sped past it.

Dracos slowed down, assuming they were taking a commercial flight, then watched as the black Mercedes drove past the airport turnoff. He followed at a suitable distance down the main highway, which gave way to country roads. The Mercedes turned into a newly laid strip of asphalt and slowed down. There were now only the two cars on the road. The Mercedes pulled into the driveway of an old airport terminal.

Julie looked through the window, 'Oh, this looks like the airport we landed at when we first came to Cyprus.'

'It is.' Peter confirmed. 'It's the old airport. Not used much these days, except for special flights, I think.'

The Mercedes pulled up right next to a small jet, its engines already running. The stairs were down and the two passengers vacated the car and ran up like VIPs, waving their thanks to Alexis.

Julie took a quick peek at the aircraft's side, noticing the flying horse logo and the word Pegasus.

Dracos watched from a distance as the plane took off, then made a call. 'They have just left on a private jet, but I will follow them as soon as I can.'

'Do it. Be smart, be quick, and get after them. I have no resources there, so you will have to improvise. Do not let me down.' The line went dead before Dracos could reply.

He checked the phone for the nearest departures from Cyprus; there were two possibilities, Heraklion in Crete or Athens. But he needed to be sure, so he waited for the Mercedes to turn around and come back down the road. He pulled over to the side as the vehicle approached, before swinging his own out, placing it in a head-on collision with the oncoming car. He slammed the brakes on, knowing Alexis would swerve to avoid hitting him.

Dracos smashed into the side of the Mercedes.

The airbag inflated, trapping Alexis who started bleeding from a cut to the forehead, but apart from that, he was fine and tried to restart the car. The engine revved, but still dazed by the incident, he could not find the pedal to accelerate away or see through the windscreen as the airbag obscured his view.

Dracos had cushioned his own impact, so he jumped out of the car quickly and climbed into the back of the Mercedes. No one was around but he was certain someone somewhere nearby had heard the crash. He pulled out his Heckler & Koch MK23 pistol, complete with silencer, and placed it on the back of Alexis head. 'I don't have time for this, so you will tell me exactly where they are going?'

'Who?' Alexis said, still dazed.

'The people you just dropped off. Where are they going?'

'I'm not sure, but someone mentioned they were flying to Crete. That's all I know.'

'Good boy, now drive me to the airport fast.'

'The car is fucked up, it won't start.'

Dracos took out his knife and cut the airbag away. 'Don't stall me, boy. This is a Mercedes, it got a bang on the side, nothing to do with the engine. Drive.'

Alexis adjusted the rear-view mirror, glimpsing the man holding the gun. He put his foot to the floor, revving the car's engine again, aware of the time he needed to get back to the airport. He gripped the steering wheel, tasting blood from his cut lip, the sweet taste dripping down his throat almost making him gag. How could he get out of this?

ABOARD THE PLANE, Julie sat in her luxurious leather chair, where she had plenty of leg room to stretch out. In fact, she had the entire plane. One woman from the previous night was the hostess, who kept busy moving up and down the aisle plying her with small crudités and glasses of Champagne.

Peter was already asleep; he had stretched out at the back and was happily snoring away.

Julie stood up, walked to the front of the plane, and peered out over the clouds.

The cabin door opened, and Mr Lukas stood before her.

'Beautiful, aren't they?' He commented. 'I have always loved clouds.'

She smirked. 'I do seem to recall that you were always pictured on a cloud.'

'Artistic license, they call it. But how else would the painters and artists portray the King of the gods, sitting on a beach or a hilltop? No, something majestic, fantastic… so that's what they came up with. I think they still do. Though, cloud sitting is not very practical.'

Julie smiled, she was beginning to like Mr Lukas, she just couldn't get used to calling him Zeus.

'At least I get to fly, but only jets these days.'

'Why are you here? We said our goodbyes this morning.'

'I wanted a word with you before we arrive.' His voice took on a serious tone. 'You must understand this, you will be the first mortal to enter the Underworld for eons, and it is a place unlike anything you know or can imagine. It is a world within a world, split into five different parts. We are uncertain where Richard is, so I hope that by the time you and my Daughter get there Persephone will know of his whereabouts. Otherwise, you may have to find him on your own, and that could be the end of you. I like you, Julie Cole, and I have much respect for your husband, but this is something beyond most mortals' understanding. I never interfere in the mortal world, so bringing you here is the best I can offer, and as far as I can go. There are many dangers you will face, all odysseys have them, which makes them so compelling to read. But yours could be fraught with a lot of unknowns, which is why I will ask one last time. Do you still want to go to the Underworld? I can turn this plane around and you and Mr Shaw can go back to your lives.'

'I have come this far, I am not turning back.'

'So be it. And Julie, whatever gods you believe in, I pray they protect you. At least as much as I have tried to do.'

'Thank you. I know I may be the first mortal to embark on this journey, but do you still have followers today? What I mean is, are there people who still worship you?'

'That is an interesting question, one that requires more than a simple yes or no answer, because it is all a matter of understanding. You told me you believe in your God without seeing Him, and now you believe in me because you have seen me, but many of my followers have never seen me but still worship in all the old ways. These people come from all over the world, with large groups in Greece, and one even has members not too far from where you were born.'

'Boston?' Julie queried, her accent noticeable.

'Near there. They practice the ancient polytheistic religion and it is their intention to carry on the old ways, our ways, but in the modern world. Their devotion is total and they have many who join regularly. The roots of this religious order cover many parts of the globe and I am sure they would be interested in your odyssey, but that is not be possible. Yet, they honour us and the old ways. They have a lovely phrase that they use. *Remember, the gods are not separate from the real world, the tangible world, but integral with it.*' He held her gaze firmly. 'This is what I mean by commitment and service. People trust in you even though they have never seen or heard you. Sounds familiar? It should, it applies across all religions.'

She had been put in her place, but gently, an admonishment for her earlier doubts and rantings about the god who now stood looking down at her.

'Excuse me, I must prepare for landing. I suggest you wake Mr Shaw.'

Standing up, she looked across to Peter, who was practically lying on the chair, his snoring loud and audible.

DRACOS PULLED himself closer to the window and pushed the gun into the boy's neck, teasing along the spine. 'How far and how long?'

'It's just ahead. Once we get past that roundabout, we are about half a mile away.' He kept his gaze firmly on the man in the back seat as the silencer probed his back. His fear obvious as his thoughts raced. *I've got to make a move soon... Run the car off the road, crash it? but how do I do it without suspicion? ram it into a tree?* He placed his foot on the accelerator, the car moving faster, much like his thoughts as he desperately sought an answer.

As the road twisted, Dracos spotted a deserted road and pointed. 'Turn there and stop the car. I will drive from here.'

Alexis did as he was told, turning off from the main airport road and pulling over to the side where several large trees and bushes camouflaged them from other motorists. The vehicle ground to a halt, his thoughts of crashing going out of his mind. Still, he had to think of another plan, and fast.

The man in the back climbed out, opened the front car door, and climbed into the passenger seat.

Alexis never saw the coil of wire as it whipped around his neck.

The homemade garrotte created a thin red line, coating the wire before a greater stream oozed from the neck as it dug through. Alexis tried to grip and pull as it sliced into the muscles, his eyes bulged, his tongue flapped, and his breathing drew to a wheeze. The white shirt was quickly smeared crimson, his black trousers equally soaked as blood flowed freely.

Dracos tightened his grip one last time. Alexis' eyes bulged again and his breathing halted. It was over in less than twenty seconds. The wire had done its job perfectly, practically cutting the young man's head from his shoulders.

Dracos pushed the limp body under the front seat, then taking up his position in the driver's seat, he reached into his airport bag and took out a white cloth. Methodically, he wiped away all traces of blood that had spurted onto the dashboard, front seat, or onto his clothing. Satisfied, he grabbed the limp body and dumped it into a clump of bushes. Gazing at the boy's body, he felt tempted to take a picture, but time was against him. He needed to be on that plane. He hurriedly cut some low-hung branches from a tree to cover the body and got back into the car. He opened his bag, took out a fresh shirt, pair of jeans, and sneakers. Dressing quickly, he climbed back into the driver's seat, and threw his own bloodied suit of clothes into the bushes. Finally, he carefully cleaned the thin wire of the garrotte. 'Don't want to cut myself.' His words conveying his callousness and total contempt for his victim.

The kid was right; the airport was just half a mile away. He eased the car out onto the main road, as a stream of airport-bound traffic overtook the battered Mercedes.

MESSENGER TO THE GODS

*J*ulie was first down the steps, then she and Peter watched as Pegasus turned on the tarmac, skirting, before taxiing down the runway again. Within seconds, she was airborne and out of sight.

The newly arrived passengers stood staring into the wide, open spaces of the empty aerodrome, a warm breeze filtering across them. Looking around, they saw their cases neatly stacked beside them, waiting. But for whom, or what?

In the distance, a small indistinct vehicle approached them slowly. As it drew closer, Julie recognised it as a Citroën C5 Dyane, its shape and design unmistakable. She cast her mind back to the time at Aldershot, several of the soldiers had had them at the barracks. She could never see the attraction, it was altogether too quirky for her.

The car trundled through the roadways, came to a stop close to where they stood, and the driver leaned out of the window.

Julie gaped. Greek god in every manner possible, he had a mop of short shaggy blond hair, a well-tanned face, and wore a tight-fitting vest which accentuated his muscles. She smiled, opened the passenger door, and sat beside the hunk.

Peter collected the cases and bags, placed some on the back seat, and the rest in the small car boot.

'Looks like I missed Dad.' The stranger said as he stared through the window. Seeing no aircraft in the sky or people on the ground, he turned to address his passengers. 'Welcome to Crete. I assume Dad told you about me. I'm Hermes, Messenger to the gods, and Zeus' number two son. But you knew that already. So, again, welcome.' His smile and flashing blue eyes were infectious.

Julie kept staring; he looked young, probably only twenty-five.

Hermes returned his gaze to his companions, uncertain what to make of them, and started the car, letting it rumble over the bumpy road. 'We will stay at my place, it's close to where we need to go tomorrow. So, here is the plan.' He spoke as he drove.

His passengers listened intently.

'Early in the morning we will go up to Dikteon, for a look around dad's cave. I will point out all the places you need to see and where to look. After we get back, you will get ready for the night excursion, away from curious tourists and guards. Don't worry, I will take care of the guards, as I know them pretty well. All they need is entertainment. The rest...' his tone became serious as he looked straight at Julie. 'This is just the beginning.'

His words momentarily took away the relaxed feeling both were experiencing, reminding them there was more than a hint of danger to come.

'But we can talk about all this in detail at my place. You must be hungry, so we'll go grab something to eat, drink some wine, and have a few beers. After that, you rest.' His jovial demeanour was back. Following a bend, he turned the bumping and trundling C5 off the side road and joined the smooth surface of the primary thoroughfare. The signpost showed Mount Dicte - 8 kilometres.

DRACOS SAT CRAMPED in the small aircraft seat. Next to him was a large Cypriot woman with enormous arms, her body on the way to becoming obese. She looked past fifty but her face well made up, with just a hint of perspiration which glowed across her cheeks and forehead. She paid no attention to her fellow passenger, reading her magazine and chewing noisily on the bag of Koupes she had purchased at the airport café. For him, it meant what little room he had was even more cramped as she shuffled her arms about while pushing the food into her mouth.

He turned away, stared at his watch, and wondered if they had found the kid's body yet. He stood up, pushed past his companion, and into the aisle, his bulky frame making it difficult for anyone to get past him, and there was an impromptu shuffle dance performed as he moved towards the vacant lavatory. Inside, he stared into the mirror. His face needed a wash and his body odour told him he needed to shower. He also needed to change his clothes again, as there were spots of dried blood on his shirt.

The aircraft banked to one side, which Dracos did not appreciate as it almost tipped him over onto the washbasin. The announcement from the cabin was for passengers to return to their seats as they were approaching Heraklion Airport. He duly obliged, opened the lavatory door, shuffled again down to his seat, and squeezed into it. The plump woman had finished her food and was busy reapplying her makeup and lipstick. Dracos did not return her smile.

THE CAR PULLED into the side of what looked like a small house. The sign outside read, 'Eat traditional Cretan food, finest on the island.' A large Olive Tree obscured the other languages on the menu.

Hermes sat in the car looking at his passengers, turning to Peter then Julie, his instructions were clear. 'Never speak my name here, people will think you are crazy. My island name is Manoussos but call me Manny, so you won't get confused. We will eat here,' he pointed. 'Try some traditional food, it will give you a taste of the island. You will find none of the fast-food places you know, as here, food is cooked traditionally, so it can take several hours to prepare. But it should all be ready by now. If you want to drink something after your long journey, the local wine Raki is best. I think we are all set. Remember, Manny.' He reminded them again as he got out of the car.

They were greeted by a jovial gentleman by the name of Psarantonis, who was dressed in a striped apron, black trousers, and a pair of sandals. He had a ruddy complexion, sported a small black moustache, no beard, and his eyes were dark. His teeth had seen better days as one of the front ones was missing, which made his smile a little humorous, but his hospitality was genuine and he made a tremendous fuss over the new guests, particularly Manny. He was probably around fifty-five and spoke English like a tourist with more than a lilt of Greek, but good enough to be understood plainly.

'These are my friends from England, Psarantonis. They are visiting the island for a few days and want to sample your delicious food.' Manny was good at flattery.

Julie knew it also worked well on the women he met because aside from his god-connection, he was also good-looking and sexy, and she would bet most women would love to have this one beside them in bed or on top of them. It was a wicked thought, and she smiled at the Greek god dressed in a vest, jean shorts, and sandals.

More locals filled the tables as their dishes arrived. First came the customary Greek salad, with some variations to the

Cypriot version; with extra olives and spices added to give it more of a tang on the tongue. The local wine Raki, which the locals drank like water, accompanied the salad. Peter opted for a chilled beer, Julie stayed with the Raki; blood red, it tasted slightly bitter, and was a complete change from the Ambrosia they had been served by Christoulides.

As they sat eating, a small group of German tourists walked in. They were young, no more than twenty, and looked like they might be students. The older people in the restaurant turned their backs on them, a rather obvious shunning that did not escape Julie, and she opened her mouth.

Hermes leaned over to her. 'Not now, I will tell you later.'

Three more of Manny's friends showed up; the group became six, then seven, then ten.

Chatter grew louder and a mix of laughter and shouting became the order of the day. The group of Germans were whisked away into a quiet corner, and for a while only the waiters remembered they were there. More dishes appeared on the table, then Raki, and beer too.

Julie smiled, laughed, dined, and drank. She was not sure what she was eating, and Manny was finding it hard to keep explaining the dishes that now littered the table. There were a lot of cheeses and olives and a dish called Dakos, which was like a baby rusk covered in tomatoes, garlic, and assorted capers and spices.

Manny waxed lyrical about this particular dish. 'This is very special. It was originally crafted in gold and given to King Minos. Inside contained the wisdom, knowledge, and imagination of Festos, which culminated in the creation of the cave of Kamares. Today, we represent it as you see here in this rusk.'

Both smiled, not sure what Manny was talking about as it would appear the wine was making its mark on his persona. However, with such an array to choose from there appeared to be no more room for the house speciality dish, Gamopilato, meaning 'rice of the wedding.'

Manny once again leaned over to Julie and shouted. 'This is the best. They usually only serve it at weddings but today they honour you. It is a mix of Chicken, Goat, and Lamb with traditional herbs and spices cooked for two to three hours in the traditional way. Delicious, and as I say, only served at weddings. So, they must think you guys are special.'

As she ate the delicious meal, she looked around the room. Could it be that the people in the restaurant knew of her plans? She put it out of her mind and tucked into the plate piled high with meat, spices, and vegetables.

WITH JUST ONE BAG, Dracos got through immigration quickly.

Then a smartly dressed customs officer pulled him aside. 'Please open your bag.' It was not a request. The officer busied himself pulling out the toiletry bag and the two wooden figures. When he noticed slight traces of blood on one of the figures, his eyes looked directly at Dracos'. 'There is blood on them?'

Dracos felt nervous, not expecting the interrogation. 'They are a gift for my Mother, hand-carved, but the chisel slipped, and it cut my finger. A nasty one, see?' He pushed his hand in front of him. There was a thin line where the wire had nicked him, though the blood was Alexis'.

'You should be more careful, Mr Dracos.'

Dracos sighed, he was one of his own men.

'Enjoy your stay and give my regards to your Mother. I have left a little something for her in your bag. Let me walk you out, the car is waiting.'

The two men walked close to each other as they left the customs hall, the officer making sure that no alarms went off as Dracos exited the airport.

Dracos moved to the car park sign and opened his bag. Inside was a brown envelope, a set of car keys, and a note that said,

Look in the glove compartment, there are also some tools in the boot for you.

It was not signed.

Dracos climbed into the Fiat, which was barely big enough for his frame and shifted the seat back as far as it would go. It still felt cramped. On the passenger's seat was a road map and a brochure for Sea Bay Apartments, but it would appear that the place was nowhere near the sea. At least it was close to the Dikteon Caves. He would wait until he was far away from the airport before opening anything else.

He pulled off the main road and into a side turning, where the car ran over a couple of deep ruts before stopping. It was a place full of olive trees, and behind them was a large escarpment of rocky crags and hills. He opened the glove box, where he found another brown envelope. There was a Glock pistol, silencer, and several bullet clips. He loaded the gun and placed it inside his jeans, covering the shape with his shirt. He reached inside the envelope again and pulled out a set of keys and a note written on the back of a compliment slip for the apartment.

His phone rang.

'Yes, Sir, I have arrived. Yes, I have the stuff I need, and I will check on the map to see where I need to go tomorrow. I'm not sure, I suspect they have… Thanks, if you can do that… Yes, I know… It was necessary… No, I don't think it will make any difference… we are in two separate countries now. Random, Sir… Needed to be done. Yes, I am sure. No, I won't… I will report back when it's over… Then…' the line cut before he could finish his sentence.

He picked up the map and turned the car around, back to the main road and with its engine labouring, it began slowly climbing the steep hill.

13

A GOOD NIGHT'S SLEEP

After much kissing from Manny to whomever he was saying his farewells to, Julie and Peter left the table and politely pushed their way through to the exit. They too were accosted, hugged, and kissed by a variety of men and women who had all turned into guests at the table and were well on their way to becoming intoxicated.

Outside, the air was still warm as the sun set.

'What do we owe you for the meal, Manny?' Peter spoke to his host.

'Nothing, the meal and drinks were free. You are our guests and how do you say… custom, won't allow it. The payment was your presence and your enjoyment. It is Cretan hospitality to treat our guests in such ways.'

Both were surprised and a little shocked but grateful. Such generosity was wonderful and welcome.

'We must move, you need a good night's rest.'

As they drove slowly away, Julie looked over to Manny. 'So why did some people in the restaurant ignore those German kids?'

'Crete was occupied by the Nazis during World War II. Many

Cretans were working with the resistance to raid and sabotage the occupation; thousands were killed, whole villages destroyed, and the people never forgot. Much like the Turks did to Cyprus in nineteen seventy-four.'

'I never knew about Crete. Something history books don't talk about a lot. Unless you were there.' Julie replied.

'History books are just the maps of time. I should know, I have lived through most of it.' In that sentence, Manny, or Hermes, confirmed his status. If there had ever been any doubt about his authenticity.

It also smacked hard into Julie's conscience. For in a moment, she had forgotten the real reason why they were here, about *perfect thought*, and what it would mean on this odyssey.

They drove the rest of the way in silence.

The accommodations were small for a god, nothing elaborate in the furnishings or décor, but at least comfortable. Most of the exterior walls were white and bleached by the sun, and the rooms inside the house were undersized. There was a kitchen/diner, the counters made from some red-coloured hardwood, two bedrooms upstairs, and a sofa in the living room, next to a small TV. There were no pictures on the walls, nothing that would link Hermes to his rich ancestry. It was a 'med' bachelor pad, with an impressive collection of empty bottles neatly stacked by the back door.

'Well, this is home, for now.' Hermes said. 'Who knows, one day I might go back to Olympus and relax there. I have to tell you, that place is unreal, statues, gods, and muses everywhere. Some parties are wild, but I haven't been back for eons. This place suits me better.'

The difference between mortal and god was obvious, as the mention of Olympus triggered once again the feelings of *can this be real?* Hermes spoke matter-of-fact, never disguised his divinity, and merely kept it as a discussion point. It felt like an illusion, but for Julie time was drawing near when all that she had heard, seen, or even dreamed was becoming authentic and soon she would need to act. The thought sent a shiver down her spine.

'You two, go get settled. I will sleep on the sofa, as you need proper rest. We will have a couple of drinks to see what we must do and I will try to explain all you need to know… well, as best as I can.'

Peter was first to wind his way up the spiral stairs. He grabbed both cases, knowing they were not heavy, but it turned out to be more cumbersome while twisting and rotating them around the staircase. Reaching the top, he shouted down. 'Which one is mine?'

'The first one on the left, I gave Julie the one with the shower.'

Climbing the stairs, Julie pushed Peter aside, took her suitcase, and planted a small kiss on his cheek before entering the second bedroom. Placing the suitcase at the foot of the bed and without ceremony, she kicked off her shoes and flopped onto the bed.

It had been a long day.

DRACOS REACHED the apartment just as the sun set. He climbed out of the car, taking the bag with him. He dug in the envelope, took out the keys, opened the door, and switched on the lights. It wasn't the most luxurious apartment but as he walked around, he noticed a set of stairs. He carried the bag up and along a passageway to the bedroom. Opening the door, it surprised him to see a large picture of the coastline with waves making their way to shore. He smiled and said aloud, 'Perhaps this is why it's called Sea Bay Apartments.'

He opened the curtains. No sign of a coastline, only mountains. He focused the binoculars and switched to night vision. Scanning the surrounds, he noticed a group of feral cats, the mother busy feeding three kittens. One was a little away from his siblings, playing with a pebble, hitting it along the ground with its paw.

Dracos opened his bag, took out the gun, twisted the silencer in position, and loaded the weapon. Deftly, he opened the window and placed himself to the side as he didn't want to be seen.

With one hand on the night vision glasses and the other on his gun, he aimed at the small group of cats. His first shot took out the mother. The second and third, two of the kittens, and with his final shot the kitten with the pebble as it tried to run and hide from the sound. This fourth shot split the fleeing kitten's head wide open, scattering its tiny brain to the earth. There were a few seconds of silence, followed by the screeching sound of cats, crying in the darkness. Dracos shut the window, pleased with his target practice. The cats continued to cry loudly, mourning their kin.

BOTH VISITORS SLEPT for a few hours, as lunch had been large and filled them up; it also made them feel lazy as noted by the time they were asleep. Now refreshed, Julie was first down the stairs, with Peter on her heels.

Hermes had set up a table with cups of black coffee, already poured for them. There were also assorted maps and brochures laid out to review.

Julie picked one up called *Zeus' Birthplace* and flicked through the pages. The images of the caverns they were to visit looked vast and daunting. With much climbing of stairs, she was sure of that.

'Good, you are checking out the brochures, but they don't do justice to the site. Dad's birthplace is impressive but the cave where his treasures are stored, including the Gorgon's head, that is magical. This will be another first for you, as no mortal has ever stepped over the threshold.' There was a sense of anxiety and wonder at the thought of these two being the first and only mortals to enter Zeus' Cave. 'Are you ready for this?' He looked straight at them.

Both nodded somewhat nervously.

'Right. So, tomorrow morning you will see the caves as tourists. Afterwards, we will come home to rest then go back in the evening. It will be dark but I got some torches so you won't walk around blind. Use them sparingly, they will not last long. After they lock the place up, you must use this key to get in.' Hermes put a key on the table. 'The place will be guarded, but I will take care of that. So, do you remember what Zeus told you?'

Julie shrugged. 'Not all that well, there was Ambrosia involved. And a lot of food and drink.'

Hermes laughed. 'There always is. Okay, I'll go over it. Once inside, go as fast as you can down to the bottom chamber. Strip off your clothes, swim to the middle of the pool, and you will be beneath *The Mantle of Zeus*, which resembles a chandelier. Shine your torch at the bottom, and watch for the beam that will direct you to the cave entrance.

'Follow the beam and swim as fast as you can. When it hits the entrance, dive under the water to about ten feet. Now, the tricky part. You need to find the symbol of a lightning bolt on the wall; it's not very clear so you must search for it. Once you find it, shine both your torches onto the mark. The light triggers a rock to roll away and you will climb inside.

'There, you will find flame torches, light them. Soaked in oil, they will flare, and help you make your way along the passageway. When you reach the end, the cave opens into a vast cavern, and ahead will be Zeus' treasure trove. Where he keeps all the things he has collected over the centuries.'

'Such as?' Julie asked curiously.

'The arrow that killed Achilles, the Golden Fleece from the

Argonauts, The Minotaur Head from Heracles' trials, the sword once used by Hector, and most importantly, the Gorgon's head, which is in a box under the table covered by sackcloth. Take that off and you will see how it works. To keep her eyes from opening, she wears a silver mask while her head is contained inside another mirrored box, so that if she were set loose, she would only see her own reflection. Be very careful, her hair is made of serpents, and these will be dormant, unless aroused. Search through the serpents on her head and cut the skin of the correct one. Do you know which one?'

'Yes, we look for the purple one and use the chalice to capture the blood.' Julie repeated what she had learnt.

'I am impressed, my Father taught you well. Once you have the blood, it will be sealed inside the chalice. Quickly make your way back to the cave door, whereupon is a stone medallion; turn it once to open. Then swim to the surface and get out of the caves as fast as you can. Unlock the gate and make your way down the hill, where I will be waiting with the car. Do you want me to go through it again?'

Julie shook her head and picked up her coffee. Peter didn't say a word.

'Oh, one more thing. Well, two actually. Always wear the eye my Father gave you; it will protect you against the guards of the cave.'

'Guards?' Peter looked at Hermes.

'Yes, sentinels. You did not think Zeus would leave his treasures unprotected? As you enter the cave there are Harpies. Have you heard of them?'

'No. What are they?'

'There are two of them, Aello (storm swift), and Ocypete (swift wing). They watch the cave and will attack without thinking. They are fast and their form is birdlike, with human faces, but as I said, the eye will protect you. Just walk by their cages and if you can, carry some meat or bread in a bag to placate them, as they are always hungry. Once past them you will meet Talos; the bronze soldier who was created on this island and is a symbol of the old world.

'He used to circle the island three times each day, warding off any would-be attackers. He was destroyed, but my Father put him back together and cast him in bronze with a physique that is perfection; he was always one of his favourites. He is invincible, save for two areas of vulnerability; he has two veins on each leg that run from his neck to his ankles, bound by a bronze nail on each ankle. If one of the nails is removed, he will collapse and become useless. Like Achilles, his ankles are also his weakest point. Wearing the eye will give you a safe passage past him. You will be fine, just make sure that the eye is visible at all times.'

'Is there anything else we should know?' Julie said.

'No, nothing else. You can relax now, enjoy your coffee.' Hermes moved over to the table, picked up his flashing phone, opened it, and read the message. 'Excuse me, Dad is calling. I will take this outside; I won't be long.'

Peter moved over to Julie, his face full of concern, his eyes conveying more than anxiety, showing genuine fear. 'Are you sure you're up to this?' His words were full of worry.

'Yes, I'm sure. How else am I going to get Richard back? If you don't want to come, its fine, you have no obligation to me.'

'No, Julie, I would not let you do this on your own. It's just that it seems so difficult, and dangerous.'

'Because I'm a woman, is that what you mean? That I'm not capable?' She was indignant, her stance deliberate.

'No, that's not what I meant, and it has nothing to do with you being a woman. God knows I've known a good many female soldiers and I have never doubted their courage or skills. But you have never trained for this. With the greatest respect, you have never fought a battle or a war, and this is going to be one.'

'I know and don't you think I realize what is at stake? Not

just for me, but for Richard, and even you. The responsibility I carry is unrelenting. Any moment could be our last, but I must do this, for all our sakes. I also think I may be the only one who can do it, so I have to try.'

The door slammed shut, and both turned around. Hermes stood by the table, a look of anxiety across his face. He clenched and wrung his hands together, as if he were deciding on his next move. He walked over to Julie and held her hand. 'I have something to tell you both. It will make your quest even more difficult, so you must decide if you want to carry on...'

'What is it, what has happened?' Peter looked directly at Hermes.

'It's about the young driver, Alexis. He has been... murdered. They found his body earlier tonight and my Father believes the person responsible could even be here already. If Hades planned it and I would not be surprised if he did, this killer is coming for you. Knowing this, are you sure you want to continue?'

Julie got up from the table, moved to the door, opened it, and stepped out into the night air. She could not stop herself from crying. The tears rolled down her face as she thought about the polite young man who in the short time she had known him had been more than a driver, he had become her friend. Now, he was dead, and she felt a deep sense of guilt upon her shoulders.

Standing alone in the night air, she looked up to the bright stars, and there appeared to be many. She reached into her jeans' pocket, took out a crumpled tissue, dried her eyes, and touched up her mascara before walking back inside.

The two men sat quietly by the table, waiting for her.

'I need to speak to my children. May I use your phone? My battery is dead.'

'No, Julie, you can't.' Hermes stood up and walked away from the table.

'Why?'

'It's too dangerous. From now on you must only keep *perfect thought* in your mind, no other distractions. If Hades senses your weakness for your children, all will be lost. You cannot jeopardize your quest with thoughts of this world, and your children are part of that. You must live and think only for the present and the tasks ahead.'

'When can I talk to them then?'

'When it's all over. When you have Richard back, then you can tell them.'

'It seems so unfair. What if I don't come back, how will they know what happened to me?'

'They will know, but it might not be the truth.'

'Just like Richard… They will be told a pack of lies and be expected to believe it. You want me to sanction this, to say go ahead, lie to my children? And for what, to protect your identities from the real world, is that it?'

Hermes sensed her frustration and wanted to assure her it would be all right, but knew he couldn't do so.

Peter stepped forward, took her hand, and squeezed it. 'I'm here and I promise to do my utmost to not let anything happen to you. And whatever it takes, I will make sure you and Richard return to your kids. Whatever it takes.'

Tears rolling down her face, she took his hand, and said through her sobs. 'Thank you.'

Was this expression of sadness for her or for Alexis? Only she knew.

Hermes opened the front door and left the two mortals alone.

14

ZEUS' CAVE

*H*ermes was the first one up and moved quietly about, so as not to disturb his guests. He looked at his watch; seven. The sun had only just begun its work for the day, casting shadows across the hills and mountains; the birds too were late with their morning song. It was as if time had overslept and the world was playing catch up.

Footsteps on the spiral staircase signalled that one or perhaps both mortals were awake and on their way down. He busied himself in his kitchen. He toasted a couple of slices of bread, opened the fridge and picked out a selection of cold meats, boiled eggs, and cheeses as well as olives. He placed the kettle on the stove and waited for it to boil, as he positioned plates, cutlery, and cups on the table.

It was Peter who appeared in the kitchen.

Oddly, this was the first time the two of them were alone, as either mortal had not been here long enough to have had time for much else but going over the plan.

'Good morning. Coffee will be ready in a minute, but help yourself to breakfast. We have an excellent selection of cheeses, bread, and meat.'

Peter sat at the table and watched as Hermes pushed plates and food towards him. He took up a knife to cut a wedge of cheese before lightly buttering the toast.

'Did you sleep well?' Hermes sensed it was the wrong question to ask, so he followed it with the pertinent one. 'Have you seen her this morning?'

Peter shook his head and took a bite from his toast.

Hermes looked outside. The sun was now working well and the warmth from its rays coated the land around the house. He sat opposite Peter, both sipped their coffees, and he said. 'Do you think she will continue?'

'Honestly, I don't know. But after what happened to young Alexis, she's scared. I'm scared. If, as you say, this killer is after us, perhaps she will give up and go home. But I don't think so. She has come this far, she will see it through, no matter the cost. If there's a chance to get Richard back, she will take it.'

'I think you are right, but again, unfortunately, there is only so much I can do to assist. I am the 'Keeper of Souls' and can guide you both to the Underworld, and although I can enter that domain, I cannot with a mortal. Please understand, we are doing things that have never been done before. Not in all the ages. This is a first for all of us.'

'You can take me too?'

'Yes.'

'I thought only Julie and Aphrodite could go into the Underworld.'

'That was the position before but with someone chasing after her, concessions need to be made. She needs all the protection she can get. In fact, both of them do. Will you go?'

'Yes, I was serious when I said I would do all I can to protect her… both of them.'

Hermes smiled and raised his hand in gratitude to the answer.

The light footfall on the stairs announced the principal character's arrival.

'Good morning, Julie.' Hermes watched as she came down the stairs.

Dressed in shorts, a white T-shirt, and had a pair of walking sneakers on, she smiled and sat at the table. 'Is breakfast still going?'

'Yes.' Hermes said.

'Great.' Her accent was showing again. 'I need it before we get going.'

Hermes couldn't disguise the wry smile that appeared on his lips. This was it, a new odyssey was about to begin. The two mortals' fates were sealed.

AFTER SHOWERING, dressing, and having a quick breakfast, Dracos pieced together the equipment he needed for the journey to Mount Dicte and the Dikteon Cave. He had done some light reading the previous night while listening to the felines mournful cries and was confident he had sufficient information about the place to strategize his next moves. He dropped maps and brochures into a small rucksack and picked up his car keys, knowing he could only drive so far up the mountain before needing to continue on foot. He opened the door to the apartment, let himself out, and slammed it shut.

A feral cat walked past him, glancing in his direction, as if knowing he was the one responsible for the slaughter of the mother and kittens, before scurrying off into the hillside and sheltering under a large tree.

Climbing into the car, he tried to adjust the seat again, but it wouldn't go back any farther. Frustrated and with his body almost hunched in the driver's seat, he started the car and began his drive towards his destination.

Hermes checked his watch. The caves were opening in thirty minutes, so he needed to drive a little slower, as he did not want to arrive too early. The situation easily remedied itself, for as they rounded the corner ascending the slope, a large tourist bus straddled the road. He could not see ahead of the bus, or sideways as there was only one lane up. The car could not speed up that quickly anyway to overtake, so he resigned himself to following at the set pace.

'How far is it now?' Julie asked.

'The bus is holding us up, but we should be there soon. Besides,' he pointed to the lumbering vehicle in front of them. 'It can't go all the way to the top, so it will let the people off so they can walk the rest of the way. Cars can ride a little further up. But it's still early, we are not pressed for time.'

Peter leaned forward from the back seat. 'Are you coming with us into the cave?'

'No, I'm going to chat to some of the guides, and set things up for tonight. You carry on, you know where to go and what to look for. Take in all that you can and memorise it, next time we come here it will be dark.'

The car laboured behind the bus as both vehicles edged closer to the mountaintop.

Farther back, Dracos was also stuck; he kept shifting gears, slowing, speeding up then slowing again as the car ascended. His patience was wearing thin, but it wouldn't help to get cranky, as ahead of him was not one but three coaches packed with tourists, and between them, he could see what looked like a large delivery truck toiling its way around the narrow mountain roads. There was nothing he could do except go with the flow.

❧

As the coach pulled over to the side of the road to allow its passengers to take photographs of the impressive scenery, the C5 accelerated past as fast as it would go.

They read the road sign, Synchro, and underneath it was a tourist symbol showing Dikteon Cave. The car wound its way upward and as it reached a sharp bend in the road, it too pulled off to the side and into a parking area.

'This is as far as we go in the car. From here, it's on foot,' Hermes said. 'Psychro means cold in English and you can see why, we are a long way up. The village is about a kilometre from here and the cave almost a thousand and twenty-five metres at the northern slopes of Mount Dicte, so I hope those are good walking shoes.' He pointed at Julie's footwear.

'We shall see.' She said, keen to get started.

'You can take a donkey ride up, if you prefer.'

'No, we're fine, on foot it is.' She didn't like the idea of a donkey ride.

'A good brisk walk will do us both good to clear our heads.' Peter stood next to Hermes and smiled; he was not looking forward to this bit at all.

'I will meet you back here in approximately two hours. Take your time going around, but make sure you see all that you need to.' Hermes stood by the car and watched the two tourists begin their climb. He took out his phone, pressed the buttons on the dial, and waited as the screen lit up. When it was answered, he said, 'They have left for the caves.' After shutting the phone, he too began the climb.

The walk up the hill was strenuous as the pathway was steep and Peter had to stop to catch his breath more than once; Julie barely paused as she strode on up. They heard voices ahead of them and a few tourists-stands appeared, selling all kinds of bricà-brac; small chalk statues of Zeus and pictures of the caves, and books in a variety of languages.

Peter caught up to Julie as she made it to a small kiosk at the entrance of the cave and handed over the admission fee Hermes had given them. This was the antechamber, and already the humidity inside was high. Ahead of them was a small party of tourists gathered around a young woman smartly dressed in a grey skirt and red T-shirt, a symbol of the sun emblazoned across her chest. She was explaining in very good English the history of the caves.

They mingled with the group and eavesdropped for a short while before moving away to negotiate the incline down the internal stairs. Stalactites hung like rock chandeliers, whilst stalagmites stood like sentries, guarding the precious memories of the cave. As they descended farther, people fanned out, some going in one direction whilst several others went the opposite way.

As seconds ticked by, they noticed the silence, as the deeper they went, the quieter their surroundings became. But for them, the only direction was down. From their vantage point, they could see small inlets in the rock walls where bats and rock doves congregated. The descent took their breath away as the air became thinner, the humidity thick, and both sweated. Peter was finding the exercise a challenge.

As they moved through the well-lit stairs and balustrades, they sensed another presence and at one point, Julie spun around quickly. There was no one she could see. Here, thoughts ran wild.

Off to the side were small niches in the rock, where sacrificial offerings had been placed. There were even remnants of crockery and vestiges of burnt offerings, as evidenced by the scorch marks on the walls.

'This must be the area they call *Temenos,* the sacred place.' Julie whispered.

'It's not far according to the guidebook, so keep going.' Peter stopped. 'Did you hear that?'

'It sounded like… never mind.' She was also getting spooked.

Possibly, they were the only ones this far down in the caves, and the rocks and echoes produced all kinds of sounds to feed overactive imaginations.

'Let's keep going,' Peter wanted to get it over with and return to the surface.

'I hear water so it can't be far.' Julie picked up the pace and moved quickly along the trestles bordering the stairs.

Peter looked at his watch. 'Can you believe we have been here almost an hour already? How time flies when you're enjoying yourself.'

Julie shrugged at the sarcasm, continued for another five minutes then pointed. 'There. Look at all the rocks surrounding the pool, the water, it's amazing. Looks blue, then turns to vivid green. Also looks quite deep… and I can see down into the water. Look at the submerged rocks… do you see them?'

'Yes, but look above you.' Peter pointed upward.

Julie stared. '*The Mantle of Zeus*… It's magnificent, and it's true, no picture does it justice. Nature created it and the gods endorsed it.' Her face glowed with wonder as she stood looking at the incredible structure. 'Absolutely amazing. Look at how the rocks are formed and how they reflect against the water and the water kicks back at them. I see it like a rock throne.'

'You could say that. Personally, I think its shape looks like a cloak, and that's what the guidebooks say. Let's go down to the pool for a better view.' Peter's enthusiasm was back.

As they moved down the last remaining steps to the base of the lake, the only sound was the pool of water lapping against the rocks. Standing close together, they looked across the water to a small chamber at the back of the cave.

'So, this is Zeus' place of birth and where his mother hid him from his Father Cronus, who apparently had an appetite for anyone who might replace him. Swallowed his children just to prevent such an outcome… Didn't help much, Zeus and his older siblings eventually killed him.' Julie pointed to the hole in the rocks.

'Aren't you quite the scholar, I am impressed.'

She took his hand, looked into his eyes, and asked. 'Do you believe we can do this?'

'I know you can,' Peter stood closer to her as both gazed up at The Mantle. 'Piece of cake, Julie, piece of cake. Now, we need to start back.'

As they turned to begin their climb, a large man with broad shoulders and muscular frame shuffled past and moved towards the pool.

Dracos cast a few glances around then watched the two climb back up the stairway before he too stepped down onto the side of the pool. He scanned the area, not leaving one crevice or crack out, before turning his attention to the huge stalactite that hung from the rock ceiling in the centre of the pool. '*The Mantle of Zeus*, is it? I'm sure my Master would love to smash it to smithereens. Maybe I'll do it for him.' His words were just for his ears, but the sentiment was aimed at all the gods.

15

UP THE WOODEN HILL

The climb back to the surface took longer than the descent; both needed to stop for a break, as the humidity was getting to them. Peter's shirt, saturated with sweat, looked as if someone had thrown water over him, and the extra pounds he carried were proving difficult to drag around.

Hermes stood waiting by the car and checked his watch for the third time in as many minutes. He was tempted to go back to the cave area to see where the intrepid duo was, but a light shower began to fall and he climbed back into the safety of the vehicle.

Emerging some fifty minutes after they had been at the pool, the weary travellers began the descent down the hill. The rain, which had become heavier, acted like a cooling shower and by the time they reached the car, both were soaked to the skin.

Hermes opened the door, and both climbed into the back seat. 'I have just the one towel, so you have to share. It's on the back window.' He started the car, and the C5 pulled away, slowly manoeuvring down the mountain road.

Peter handed the towel to Julie, who began drying her hair, face, and legs, before handing it back.

'You saw everything you needed to see?' Hermes said.

'Yes. The place is magnificent and the pictures only tell half the story. There is definitely a mystique about the place.' Julie said keenly.

'Good, no problems then. Anyone follow you?'

'We only saw one man who looked a bit suspicious. Arrived just as we were leaving but he never spoke so he might be a foreigner. Big guy, muscular, didn't really see his face when he walked straight past us as we started going up the stairs.' Peter replied as he slumped into the back seat.

Julie followed and dropped her head against his shoulder.

Hermes watched them through the rear-view mirror. Those two were getting closer by the minute. 'We will be home soon,' he said, before turning the ignition on.

He deftly manoeuvred the narrow roads, passing a group of labouring coaches and buses heading to the caves. The drive down was a lot easier than the one up, less traffic and steep descents pushing the C5's engine to its limits as the bends became sharper and windier.

When they joined the two-lane road close to the house, Hermes spoke again. 'After all that, you must be hungry. I will make us lunch and then you rest. You got a taste of how difficult the journey will be, so get some sleep. You need to be well prepared for what lies ahead. We will leave after dark.' He was unsure if they heard him because when he looked in the mirror again, both were fast asleep, Peter snoring loudly.

Dracos too had seen all he needed to know and returned to the entrance. The next time he saw them again he would be kitted for action, as a plan was already half-formed in his head for the next part of this adventure.

He left thirty minutes after Hermes, driving leisurely; there was no need to rush. As he went down the mountain road, he took in the scenery, which was stunning; the backdrop to Mount

Dicte impressive with the clouds rolling in to cover the peak like soft white cotton wool.

~

BACK AT THE HOUSE, Hermes pulled alongside the back door, parked, and the sudden jolt woke his two passengers from their car ride slumber. Both climbed out wearily, but once inside, they settled down.

Hermes made coffee and took out a pile of sandwiches from the fridge. His guests, understandably, did not have much to say, merely munching and enjoying the warm liquid. He imagined both were pondering about what was to come next and preparing themselves for it.

First to speak was Peter. 'Thanks, I needed that. Now, I'm off to get forty winks.' He climbed up the spiral staircase.

'What's forty winks?' Hermes was curious at the expression.

Julie smiled at the handsome god. 'It means to take a nap or sleep for a short time.'

'I have never heard this before.' Hermes studied her. 'And it seems you need your forty winks too.'

'I know, and I am just up the wooden hill to get some.'

'Wooden hill?' Hermes looked confused.

'I will tell you later.' She planted a soft kiss on his cheek.

Perhaps this was the first time a mortal kissed him, as he could not recall another. He followed her up the stairs with his eyes, smiled, and mumbled under his breath, 'Mortals... I don't think I will ever understand them.'

~

DRACOS RETURNED to the apartment and drank a glass of wine before he sat down to call Hades.

The phone rang once.

'Yes, sir… I went today. Tonight, sir. Why do you think…? I see… and I am ready. I have all I need to finish the job. I will be back with you by tomorrow evening. Yes, I am sure… Yes, sir… Thank you.' At least he could finish the call this time. He sat back in his chair, drank the wine remnants and walked over to the sofa. Dropping himself into it, he pulled a blanket over himself and shut his eyes. The bag with the loaded Glock, he kept beside him.

PETER FOUND it difficult to fall asleep, turning one way then the other. He puffed his pillow before sinking his head back into it. The curtains were open, but the room was dark, and he could tell the afternoon light was fading. He tried again, forcing a yawn, but nothing. His body would not relax. As he lay with his eyes shut, he heard the bedroom door open. He opened them and sat up as Julie tiptoed towards him.

She smiled and sat on the bed. 'I can't sleep.'

'Nor I,' Peter said.

She pulled the covers back, seeing he was wearing just shorts. 'I need a cuddle, can I get in with you?'

Peter nodded. 'Sure.'

'Always the gentleman,' Julie smiled warmly then fixing her eyes on him, did something he did not expect. She got up from the bed, reached her fingers under her T-shirt, dragged it up, and stood in jeans and bra. Her skin shone a warm golden brown.

Half confused and half curious, Peter watched as she stared back at him; her eyes wide open, a deep sense of lust emanating from her. He couldn't help but sense it too.

Her hands moved to the top of her jeans, undid the button slowly, eased the zip down and let them fall to the floor, leaving her barely covered in her bra and a pair of G-string panties.

If this was a planned seduction, it was working.

She slid into the bed. 'Hmm, that's better. Now, hold me.' She commanded and moved her body against his chest, while one hand travelled down to nestle on the top of his underpants. 'I am so glad you came with me.'

'What are you doing? This is…'

'Just cuddle me, hold me close. Closer. That's it.'

He smelled her perfume, heard her breathing, and felt her hand as it slowly tugged and pulled down his pants.

Deftly, her fingers reached down for his manhood.

'Huh, Julie, this is… not right. Stop.' His head said no, but his body, not so much, as he felt the shaft of his cock grow as she began to rub it slowly. 'Julie, I mean it. No…'

Her hand stiffened, gripped tighter, and she leaned down to his ear. 'Take my bra off.'

He obeyed instantly. He also hoped he remembered how as it had been too long. What he did know was that his resistance was evaporating fast. Her bra slipped away, and he stroked her bare breasts before moving his head down to suck on her nipples. She moved her face down towards his now throbbing manhood, placed her mouth over it, and blew softly, before opening her mouth and guiding it down to his now erect cock. Her tongue played with the flesh and he writhed over the bed as the sensations mounted. She too reacted to his touch as he tugged at her G-string, pulling them away from her and with some urgency opened her legs before pushing two fingers into her. She gasped as he turned his fingers slowly inside her, seeking her pleasure button.

She stopped her sucking, moved to his mouth, and began kissing it, all the time telling him how much she needed this, how she had had no relations with anyone since Richard's death, and how she wanted to feel him inside her.

Peter responded. 'I have fucked no one for years either. Sheila cut me off sexually, I need this as much as you.' He said as he let his body touch hers. She opened her legs wide, pulled him down to meet her eagerly, and with grand passion let him inside her.

Hermes entered the room with a cup of coffee.

Julie walked in right behind him and her Boston accent exploded. 'What the fuck is going on here?'

Peter turned, his cock still inside whom he thought was Julie. As he turned back, he realized the woman was no normal woman but Aphrodite. His passion bare, he gaped at Julie, and felt shame at his betrayal of her.

Julie stormed out of the room.

Naked, Peter stood up and shouted after her. 'I'm sorry, Julie. So sorry.'

Now fully transformed, the naked goddess lay on the bed taunting him. 'Aren't you going to finish what you started? Come on, you need it more than I do.' Her mocking carried down the passageway.

Pulling on his underpants, Peter ran to Julie's room and banged on the door; his eyes full of tears, fear, and hatred for himself, 'Julie, Julie,' he continued to plead.

She did not answer him.

'Julie, please.' He slumped to the floor beside her door.

He waited five minutes before getting up and walking back to his room. He stared at the crumpled bedsheets, ugly evidence of the mess. He straightened them out; if only it was this easy to do with Julie.

Julie dressed slowly. She had not cried; it was just disappointing, because now, she had no idea if she could trust him again. Her affection for him had been destroyed, seeing him as just another pawn in the game they were playing; a game that was becoming ever more serious. She opened the door and walked down the spiral stairs to the living area.

Hermes sat on a wooden chair by the table, Aphrodite stood looking out of the window, but Peter had not emerged yet.

'Had your fun, did you?' Julie asked.

Aphrodite came across from the window and looked down her nose at the mortal. Before turning, she looked directly at Julie. 'I did, and it was most enjoyable, until we got interrupted. But I think it shows that he likes you.'

Julie could barely hold her temper.

'Which must be good, as you will go into battle together. But let me ask, are you sure you still want to take him? One thing is certain, he can't be trusted. A loyal friend would have refused your advances, I mean, my advances. He didn't. He lusted for you.'

Julie had been battling confusing thoughts, feelings even, but with Aphrodite's revelation, these were becoming more profound. 'All you ever do is trick people because you can't get anything done as yourself. I know you tried it with Richard too, but it didn't work, so you tried it again with Peter.' She was seething.

'Ah, but with Peter it did work. He wanted you, and was willing to sacrifice your friendship to satisfy his carnal desires. You call that a friend?'

Hermes poured a coffee. Things were getting out of hand. He must do something. 'No one is at fault here, it was my idea.'

'What?' Julie's anger rose sharply. 'Yours, why?'

'For a laugh. I am known for it, and Aphrodite knows what I am. All gods have their little traits and foibles, and mine are to play tricks on people. Sorry, this one got out of hand.'

Peter's footsteps echoed on the stairs. 'I heard all of that. You played a joke to see if I'd take the bait, and I did. But not because of whatever you two have in your heads… I do love this woman.'

Silence fell across the room.

Julie stood up from the chair. 'What do you mean, Peter?'

'I'm sorry. I have tried holding it in for a long time but can't anymore. I do love you, probably always did, right from the day we went in the helicopter together. I've always seen you as something special but never dreamed that we would become close. So making love to you, or what I thought was you, was the best thing that has happened to me in years. I am only sorry it wasn't you.'

The brief speech hit Julie like a thunderbolt. Not expecting anything like this, she now had no words to answer and stood quietly looking at the room's occupants. She studied them, dissecting their emotions, trying to guess who would say something that would make sense. She turned away, contemplating her thoughts, and walked back up the stairs.

Peter slumped in the chair. His confession had drained him.

Aphrodite walked over to Hermes. 'It seems your little joke has backfired. Now, what are you going to do? There isn't much time left.'

Hermes shrugged, aware of the timetable; he just had not expected such drama. But being the joker in the pack, sometimes the joke fell on you. This was one of those times.

In her room, Julie took a small holdall from under the bed and filled it. She packed an extra set of clothes, a vest, and the torch Hermes had given her. She also wrapped the chalice in a plastic waterproof bag, grabbed a few morsels of dried food from the small side table and an apple, and zipped the bag closed. She twirled the eye-necklace around her neck, making sure it was visible. It was odd but all she could think of was *perfect thought*, all other distractions she cast away. She opened the bedroom door and walked down the stairs.

The others sat around the table. Hermes was full of remorse. Aphrodite had a wry smile on her face. And Peter wore the mask of self-delusion, thinking, how did he ever imagine he had a chance with her?

The stairs creaked as she entered, and all three turned, waiting for her to speak.

'I'm ready. Time is getting on so if you are coming go get yourself ready.'

Her words rang around the room and signalled action. No one else spoke, Peter stood and ran up the stairs. Hermes picked up the car keys and fondled them in his hands. Aphrodite said nothing, not having expected this response. Mortals… she could never make them out.

16

ZEUS' CAVE: PART TWO

*T*here was no more time for *will she, won't she?* The die was cast and there was only one way to proceed, get to Zeus' cave, and quickly.

Night was already falling like a black cloak across the mountains. It seemed much darker than usual, the street lamps giving sparse illumination as they could only expose a limited part of the road. The C5 began its climb back up the hills. The two passengers sat together on the back seat.

Hermes drove steadily, keeping to the narrow roads, but checked the rear-view mirror regularly, in case they were being followed. A set of lights trailed in the distance behind him, but were a long way off, so they might not be significant. He turned around to face his passengers, 'We are approaching. I will stop and go make sure that all is set up. Give it ten minutes before you follow me.'

Both readied themselves for the task ahead.

When they arrived at a cluster of lights from the nearby village and the floodlit entrance to the mountain climb, Hermes stopped the car, got out, and opened the back door.

Both got out into the clammy night air. The moonlight was

opaque, but the streetlights and floodlights from the bottom of the hill were enough for everyone to see. Perhaps even a little too much.

Hermes shook Peter's hand, kissed Julie on the cheek, and told them, 'οοἴθι εὐτυχής! / Εὐτυχῶς', before explaining, 'in my language, one of the ancients, it means good luck. Oh, and remember this, even your shadow leaves you in the dark.' He turned away and began walking up the mountain road, hoping as he did, they understood he was telling them to stick together.

Opening the car boot, Julie took out her small bag, hoping that what she had brought along was what she needed.

Peter followed. Neither spoke and both checked their watches. It was just after nine. So far, they had seen no one else.

Further down the road, Dracos was parking his vehicle. He had changed into his wet suit, but worn sandals while driving, intending to change into rubber shoes once in the cave. He too had a small plastic bag. Inside, he had his loaded gun, and on the back seat was a leather belt which held his scimitar. He was ready.

Peter set off, with Julie in tow.

They kept to the path which was lit in places and in complete darkness in others. Perhaps the bulbs had blown and not been replaced. Peter shone the torch to check their footing. They continued up the hill gingerly, each step carefully measured. Approaching the entrance, they saw no guards. The large iron-gate normally locked and bolted was open, eliminating the need to use the key Peter had in his pocket. That was suspicious. Could someone else be inside?

Peter entered first, shining the beam to pierce the darkness, lighting up the room instantly. He gave the torch a slight shake, knowing he had to use it sparingly, before turning it off.

It became almost pitch black, but as their eyes adjusted, they noticed a glow coming from below. Both edged their way along the passage to the first set of stairs, holding tight onto the railing.

Earlier, the heat in the cave had been bearable, but tonight, a cold air-flow had intensified and they needed to add to their clothing to combat the chill.

Silently, they edged their way down to the next set of steps, both filled with the eerie sense that someone or something was listening in as they meandered slowly downwards.

Peter paused.

'Why have we stopped?' It was the first words she had spoken since they started the drive.

'Shh. This is where the cave splits, I need to use the torch to check where we are.' Peter turned the light on.

All manner of flying things appeared, followed by screeching and screaming, some even flying close to their faces while they crouched on the ground, trying to hide.

'Turn it off.' Julie shouted.

Bats homed in on the light and attacked even as Peter grappled with it. He covered his face and eyes with his hands as best he could, yet they swooped down again and again, screeching and scratching at both of them. He flung his body across Julie, protecting her from the attack. Scratches across his back oozed blood as random bright beams flashed across the walls. He fumbled to grasp the torch as the attacks intensified before finally locating it on the ground and hitting the off button. The shrieks subsided and the flying mammals returned to their fissures, the only audible sound the flapping of wings.

Julie looked at Peter who stood bleeding from his face, hands, and back. Luckily, her cuts were superficial, so she used a tissue to wipe them away. She offered it to him, but it wouldn't be much use. He needed bandages. 'I will clean them when we get to the water.'

He grabbed a T-shirt from his bag and mopped up the crimson tracks. 'Thanks, I'll be fine.'

Carefully, they moved down the trestle, the last major route before they came to the pool. As they edged their way down, he covered the torch with the bloodied T-shirt and shone enough light for them to see ahead; the stairs felt wet as they inched closer to the bottom, and now they could already hear the water lapping against the rocks.

Reaching the bottom, Julie moved quickly to soak her spare T-shirt in the water, and turned to Peter to bathe his wounds.

'You need that shirt when we come back.'

'It's ok, I'll swim in my underwear and leave my clothes here.' She said and stripped.

Peter mopped himself again and taking off his own clothes followed her into the water.

'I have my torch. Jesus, this water is cold.' She shivered as the icy liquid bathed her skin.

Both swam to the centre of the pool and stared up at the majestic *Mantle of Zeus*. It was impressive, a true miracle of nature. Sinking further into the pool, they began to tread water, until both were ready to aim their torches at the Mantle.

'On three.' Peter said.

'This better work, I am freezing my ass off here.' Her accent was as pronounced as ever.

'One, two, three.' They whispered together.

The beams switched on simultaneously, the light heading towards the centre of the structure. As they hit, another beam streaked brightly from the 'Mantle' and pointed downwards to about ten feet below the water. It was a clear green light, almost neon.

Julie dove first, swimming towards it. Peter followed, his body feeling the cold as his legs cramped. Julie shone her torch, but as she reached the wall and searched for the symbol, she couldn't see it. She surfaced for air, Peter close behind.

'Did you see it?' Her face showed signs out of panic as she puffed out her lungs.

'Not yet, let's go again.' Peter urged.

Julie nodded.

Launching themselves off the wall, they descended to the area where the beam still shone and pointed the torches at the spot where they assumed the symbol was. They were rewarded with success, as the light caught the image of the thunderbolt. A gap in the wall opened slowly, and as the beam filtered its light through, it opened wider. A slight incline allowed them to slide down into the cave.

Dracos, less than five minutes behind them, had put on his infra-red goggles to get down the stairs quickly, using stealth to keep a good distance between himself and his quarry. He did however stop momentarily, to see the residue spots of blood where the bats had feasted on Peter. Reaching the bottom of the cave, he could see the bright light emanating from the *Mantle*. Making sure he was not seen, he slipped into the water, dove under the *Mantle*, and came up where the cave was still open. He scanned the opening and slipped inside, before the cave closed behind him. He hid himself from sight.

Peter looked around, 'Hermes said we would see flame torches once inside. I don't see any, do you?'

'Not yet, so we probably need to go further in. We could use our torches… I'm just not sure how long mine will last. Why didn't I bring extra batteries?' Julie admonished herself for lack of preparation.

'Maybe next time.'

The wisecrack brought a smile to her face.

Peter smiled back. *Perhaps not,* he thought.

They moved another fifty yards and somewhere ahead screeching sounds floated towards them; not loud but reminiscent of bird calls. As the walls narrowed, they moved along slower.

With wet skin and in just her underwear, Julie was not dressed for a hike. She hoped the torches appeared soon. The darkness produced and multiplied sounds, because not only did they pick up screeching but also slow mechanical grinding noises that echoed across the walls.

The ground beneath their feet became less rocky, then turned to sand. As they looked around, they finally saw the torches protruding from the wall; all were unlit, but as Julie approached, the eye around her neck became bright. She held it in front of one of the torches on the wall and instantly lit them all. They gave off a bright blue, almost fluorescent flame, lighting the whole cave, so they could see the way ahead.

As Peter turned, he noted that as soon as they passed the light, the flames went out. Curious, he walked back again, the flames relit. He moved away from them and they went out. 'Julie, Julie,' he whispered.

She stopped and turned around. 'What?'

'Watch this.' He repeated what he had done, showing how the flames lit, went out, and relit, depending on where he stood. 'This is brilliant, watch.' He did it again, only this time, he began singing the Hokey Kokey. As he put his right leg in, then out, the light went in tandem with him.

'Yes, Peter, fantastic. Can we continue now?' Julie said and stifled a laugh.

Dracos watched from a safe distance, unable to fathom what the man was doing jumping backward and forwards.

The bird-like sounds grew louder, echoing throughout the cave, and as Julie drew closer, she could see a large metal cage. Inside was a large tree with branches that spanned well outside the bars. She moved slowly, knowing what to do as she edged her way towards the upcoming challenge.

The two Harpies sat on a tree branch, ready to strike. They flapped their wings, their wingspan enormous, and as their talons flexed and gripped the branch, no one would be mistaken about their power; those would rip a person to shreds if ever they got loose.

Opening her soaked bag, Julie took one of the plastic bags

containing the food and rolled some meat pieces into her hand. Holding up the blue-eye, she tossed the pieces onto the cage floor.

The Harpies swooped down to pick up the morsels.

Still holding the eye in her hand, Julie took another step. 'Hermes said there were only two, but over there, I see a third one.' She edged even closer for a better look.

The creatures eyed her with suspicion but did not approach, respecting the power of the eye that she held in her fingers.

'What are you doing?' Peter tried to pull her back.

'It's okay, they won't touch me as long as I'm wearing this.' She paused before moving forward, coming to almost touching distance of them.

This was the first time in centuries a mortal had been this close to these creatures.

'Here,' Julie threw the apple into the cage, knowing both would go for it and it would give her and Peter enough time to pass by.

What she did not suspect was that the third one would swoop down to snatch the apple from the other two. A screaming fight ensued as the Harpies tussled over the precious fruit.

'Smart thinking, Jules.'

She had not been called that for a long time and quite liked it. Together, they hurried past the cage, and as the torches went out behind them, a new set ignited ahead of them. In the flames, they could see a figure shimmering in the light, but as they drew nearer, they realized the sheer size of it. The clanking sound became louder as the creature turned its head to look down at them. Both froze as the torches shone brighter.

The glow picked out and bounced reflections from the metal body of Talos, who stood some thirty-feet tall, dwarfing the two mortals, who clung to each other as they stared up to the mechanical sentry.

Standing in the half-light, Julie stepped forward, again holding the blue-eye in her hand, showing it to the metal giant.

His head creaked as his neck turned, his body twisting towards the woman, then moved forward, his legs and thighs bent slightly as his foot placed a huge footprint in the sand next to both of them.

Will he let us continue or is this his way of stopping us? Peter wondered.

The magnificent automaton stood still, peering down at them, before slowly moving aside, allowing them to shuffle past. His sheer size alone was so impressive that there was no doubt why he had been chosen to guard Zeus' treasures. Passing by Talos, they were clear, and on their way to the treasure trove and the Gorgon's head.

MYTH AND MORTALITY

Dracos had kept a safe distance from his prey. He had no torches lighting his way but it made no difference, his night vision goggles was all he needed to pursue the targets. He could hear the screaming and screeching Harpies some distance away and as he drew nearer, the noise grew louder, reaching pitches that hurt his ears. He looked down, noticing the rocky cave floor giving way to a sandy surface.

Dropping to his knees, he crawled stealthily, then unzipping his wetsuit, he took out the Glock from its plastic bag. As he drew closer, the screaming stopped, an eerie silence falling upon the cave. Through his goggles, he watched as the creatures took their positions, ready to attack. He edged closer, the gun in his hand.

Detecting another presence in their domain, and one that should not be there, the Harpies moved to the back of the cage, the trees offering some cover. They waited briefly, sensing their quarry was close, then ventured out of their hiding place.

Using the element of surprise and with the silencer firmly attached, Dracos pumped two shots into the neck and head of the first Harpy. It screamed and collapsed. Her companion rushed to pick her up; the third and fourth shot hit the shoulder and back of its head. There was no sound, and Dracos moved closer to check that both were dead.

The third Harpy slammed her body against the cage, screamed wildly, and stretched to reach her companions' killer. And in doing so, one of his huge talons got stuck and clung to the gate as it clawed in vain at the attacker.

Dracos emptied the rest of the bullets into her body. Then, while it was still suspended on the fence and with blood dripping from its wounds, he took out his scimitar and sliced the clinging talon from its body with one blow. Picking up the blood-drenched digit, he ran a finger along its edge; it was exceptionally sharp. Carefully, he wrapped it in the plastic bag he had kept the gun in. The Harpy took one last breath and its body slumped against the iron-gate.

Dracos walked past the self-created carnage, reloaded his weapon, and focused on the path ahead. Moving stealthily along the floor while keeping his movements to a minimum, he drew closer to the light emanating from the passageway. There was Talos, in all his glory. He had read all about this man of Bronze, defeating him was going to be the hardest part of the whole exercise.

He sat on the sand with his goggles on, looking around for something he might use to rout the giant; if he couldn't do that, his mission was over. He moved back towards the Harpies' cage; there were a few pieces of iron which had been broken off but nothing too promising. He shuffled past the Harpy hanging on the gate. The other two still lay where they had fallen. He scanned the floor. There was nothing he could use as a lever, but in one cage he found a large chain that had probably been used to keep the Harpies under control. Thick and rusty, it had not been used in ages but was about twelve feet long. It was anchored to a wall on the other side of the cage with a bolt which looked somewhat weakened from years of tugging. He looked around again and found the perfect leverage tool, a long-discarded metal bar to prise the bolt open. It was not as easy as he imagined. Using all his weight and muscle, he eventually shifted the bolt until it gave way and the chain fell to the ground with a large clanking sound. It was then he heard the first footsteps of Talos approaching.

Dracos hid in the corner as the bronze hulk cast its shadow towards him. With the chain free, he slowly dragged it towards the massive being.

Talos could hear the movement but was not sure where the sound was coming from.

Dracos used the tree as cover as the giant moved closer, the clanking sound of his muscular form giving little away what direction he was moving. Dracos continued to drag the chain towards Talos, who was now within ten feet; in his hand, he carried a short sword and wrapped around his arm was a brass shield. The chain was now pulled almost all the way across. It was just a question of waiting for the right moment to strike.

Talos surveyed the ground, sweeping his glistening sword from side to side.

Dracos had one chance to get it right, but he needed the giant to turn. Grabbing the skull of a cow that had been picked dry by the Harpies, he hurled it towards the front of the gate where it smashed against the iron bars.

Talos moved towards the sound and stepped forward, following the movement, his hand swishing the sword back and forth.

Dracos ran with the chain and seeing the protruding nail in the heel, pushed a link over the nail's head and secured it. Running back to the tree, he wound the chain around one of the fallen trunks.

Talos turned, and as he did, the nail in his ankle began to slowly retract. Sensing he was becoming trapped, he turned his body sharply, only exposing more of the nail. His body glowed, first a rich reddish colour then orange and finally a brilliant vivid white that ignited and scorched the surrounding ground. The giant struggled to turn one way then the other to cut the chain, while the nail was becoming looser and he felt his strength waning.

The sheer flame intensity radiating from the metal body made Dracos cover his face with his hands to stop his eyes from burning. The chain still held tight, but for how long? The metal chain scorched, and it too glowed white. If the nail did not come out soon, the chain would melt through.

Talos tried to turn to cut the chain, but this last body twist sealed his fate. The nail popped from the heel and molten steel flowed freely. His legs buckled and he dropped his sword. As his knees gave way and he knelt on the floor, his shield cracked wide open. The trail of his lifeblood now filling around him in a pool of molten brass, his body melted slowly beneath him.

Dracos came from his safe hideout to watch the last throes of the giant automaton as it sank into the sand.

THE TORCHES CLOSEST TO ZEUS' cavern shone brighter than the ones in the passageway, and the noises that reached them were muffled because of the sheer size of the place. Behind them, they could half-hear cranking and clunking metallic sounds as Talos moved through the cave.

Peter and Julie navigated a slight incline before dragging themselves in and rolling down into the inner sanctum. Taking the lead, Peter switched on the battery torch and the sight that greeted them was indescribable; no words could match the sheer enormity of the cave and the riches it held. It was truly an Aladdin's cave.

Inside stood a stone table about twenty feet long, and on it sat many treasures. There was Paris' arrow, the one that had killed Achilles, Hector's sword, the club of Heracles, pipes of

Pan, and the teeth of the Hydra. Above them, hanging from the wall, was the Minotaur's head, and off to the side in a small enclave, a Ram's fleece. Stacks of diamonds and gems piled high, glittered against the golden shields and helmets, which were sprinkled throughout the table so there was a permanent glow.

Julie stared around her, mesmerized by the sheer wealth. But not forgetting the reason for being there, she ducked under the table. Moving further along on her haunches, she caught sight of the box covered in sackcloth. Kneeling, she gingerly pulled it and carefully guided it out from under the table. 'Is this it?'

Peter glanced over as she stood holding the box in her hands, before placing it on the table with some care. Both were apprehensive about what to do next.

Rummaging in her bag, Julie took out the silver cup that would hold the blood and placed it next to the box. Looking among the treasures, she caught sight of a small fruit knife. She pulled the cloth away. The box shimmered as it caught reflections of diamonds and flame alike, giving the cave an even brighter glow. Just for a moment, she stood staring at this wonder of the ancients, feeling humbled by its utter majesty and magic. Grasping the knife, she slid the top panel off. Seeing the Gorgon's scalp in plain sight sent a shiver down her spine that made her tremble.

'Do you want me to do it?' Peter volunteered.

Julie shook her head, not wanting to speak, to not disturb her concentration. The mirror glass of the box shimmered in the torchlight. 'Perfect thought,' she whispered under her breath.

Peter took a few steps away and watched as she began filtering through the snake hair on the Gorgon's head with one hand, while holding the knife in the other.

She parted the serpents with one finger, so she could discern the colours. Peeling them away from their coils, she unwrapped a large one. The flesh was cold and limp, and as she moved the heads away, she glimpsed the purple serpent.

Holding the cup, she got Peter to place his hand between the bunches of snakes that were grouped around it. Pushing his hand into the mess of limp snakes, he gently peeled them away so she could get a clean cut. Her hand trembled as she delved into the cold flesh, before making a slit in the skin with the knife.

As blood flowed slowly from the wound, she held the cup to the incision. It opened, taking in the precious liquid, which was almost black. It seemed like hours as they waited for it to fill, then it slammed shut. Almost reverently, she placed it on the table.

As they turned to walk away, Dracos stood in front of them.

Peter picked up a sword and moved towards the intruder. 'Who the fuck—' He did not finish his sentence or get far.

Dracos shot him twice; once in the chest and the second in the neck.

Peter crashed to the floor, the open hole in his chest letting his blood spill across the floor.

'What have you done? Peter, Peter.' Julie screamed in shock. 'Who are you?'

'I don't have time for explanations, so just give me the Gorgon's head.' Dracos eyed her up and down as he pointed the gun at her. *Amateurs, and why is she in her underwear?*

Julie stood with her hands behind her back resting on the table, staring at the stranger who had ruthlessly cut down Peter. She wanted to go to him, to hold him, to cradle him in her arms. But this bastard stood between them.

'I've come a long way, following your every step, so I don't have time for this. Once I have the Gorgon's head, all I need to do is take care of you. But before you join your friend...' He looked her up and down again and grimaced. 'I think I will have some fun. Looks like you are dressed for it.'

She understood him all too clearly. For a mere second, she

fumbled with the box behind her back. If she got it wrong, she was doomed too. 'You want the Gorgon's head?'

'No more fucking around, bitch. Give it to me.' He grunted, real menace in his words, and pointed the gun straight at her head.

'Then TAKE IT.' She yelled, spun the head around to face him, pulled off the Gorgon's mask, and held it up.

Nothing happened.

Dracos took a step forward, then stopped. As the Gorgon's eyes slowly opened, the brilliant emerald gaze fixed on him and glistened into a golden rainbow. He watched mesmerised as the serpents began to slowly, rhythmically, and hypnotically undulate.

Julie held the head tight, knowing she dare not look or let go as the now roused snakes swayed to-and-fro.

Held in the grip of the Gorgon's gaze, Dracos could not move. He tried to pull the trigger but his finger, like the rest of his body, tightened; his arms felt heavy and his legs lost all feeling, as the muscles stiffened.

The Gorgon blinked, not once but twice, and the colour in her eyes went from emerald green to a vivid translucent purple. Her face lit up into a beaming smile, then a sinister glare brought the full force of her power onto her victim; his legs solidified, then his arms and face followed. Skin hardened and changed colour. Flesh turned to stone, he was no longer human, merely a statue; just another possession.

Julie shoved the head back into the box and put back the mask.

The snakes stopped writhing and settled into their original positions.

Julie pushed the glass mirror over the top of the box, before scrambling for the sackcloth to cover it. Out of breath, she stood gaping at the stone figure of her adversary, surmising he must be young Alexis' killer. Her temper was all but lost as her anger and hatred for this killer seethed.

She picked up Hector's sword, holding it in her two hands, and with all her might brought it down onto the solid figure. The blade smashed into the stone head, splitting it wide open, and she slashed and sliced wantonly, tears streaming down her face until there were hundreds of pieces lying at her feet. She sat down, panting, staring at the surrounding mayhem, then looked for something to cover Peter with.

It was then she spotted the fleece on the incline and ran across to pick it up. Could this be the fabled Golden Fleece, the one that was believed to possess power to bring back the dead? True or not, she had to give it a shot. Throwing it over Peter's limp body, she then cradled it between them and prayed for a miracle. 'Zeus, if you are listening, show me the power of *perfect thought* and bring Peter back to me.'

As her plea echoed through the cave, she closed her eyes.

The fleece took on a new life. Where it had been dirty and ragged it now shimmered in a thousand different shades of gold, the light so penetrating, she could not open her eyes. There was a radiance and feeling of incredible power emanating from the ram's skin that conveyed intense energy as it continued glowing brighter until… It stopped.

Julie sat up, staring at Peter. Did it work? She could not tell, but he wasn't moving. Sinking her head onto his chest covered by the dirty fleece, she felt it rise. *He's breathing again, he's alive.*

His eyes opened and stared at her.

She leaned forward and kissed him, a soft passionate kiss, a lover's kiss.

'Wow, that was worth getting shot for.' Peter's cool, wicked grin confirmed he was all right.

Julie held him in her arms. She was not alone anymore.

18

ODYSSEY: PART TWO

They held each other for what seemed an eternity, but was probably only a minute, proving just how far they had come.

Getting his breath back gradually, Peter looked around the cave and at the fragmented statue that had once been their ruthless enemy. Now, it was just a pile of chunks of stone. If proof was needed of Julie's determination to complete the odyssey, this was it. And if that man was Alex's killer, then his own destiny had already been determined. Julie helped him to his feet as he was still groggy, giving him a few moments to adjust to the world of the living again. After gathering their things, they took one last look around and made their way to the entrance of Zeus' treasure trove.

Outside, they followed the torches, before coming upon Talos' crushed and crumpled body. Both paused, checking the once majestic figure for signs of life. There were none.

Passing Talos, they arrived at the cages and the dead Harpies. The larger of the group, called Calaeno, or Dark, had once been a worthy guardian. Now, the body dangled pitifully from the grate, its weight moving the gate back and forth to produce a barely audible creaking sound. The rest of the scene was self-explana-tory. There was no need to stop. They moved swiftly down the pathway and onto the rocky ground.

Gaining access to the outside required the blue-eye; Julie held it in front of her. Strapping their bags to their bodies, they watched as the cave opened slowly and the sound of water reached them. They waded in, noticing the water was warmer than before, but neither cared, they wanted to be outside again.

Surfacing from the cave, Julie swam towards the area nearest the steps. Peter followed, gaining strength with every stroke he took. Both climbed onto the rocks and changed into their fresh clothes. Peter's shirt was stained with his blood from the bat attack, but at least it was dry. Slowly and carefully, they made their way up the steps, hoping as they did their torches still had enough power to get them to the surface.

HERMES CHECKED HIS WATCH. They had been gone a long time, much longer than he expected. What if something went wrong? He had imbibed a fair amount of wine and beer, then decided he had had enough and left his companions to continue on their own. 'I will give it another ten minutes before I go look for them inside.' He muttered as he meandered his way to the entrance.

But even as he considered whether to stay put or go in search of his wards, they were approaching the area where the bats had attacked them. Julie crawled along the floor, not willing to chance another bloody encounter. Peter covered the torch with his T-shirt to diminish the light, and he too crept past the flying mammals' sleeping place. Loud cries came from above and they lay still on the steps, before moving forward step by step until they were clear of the site.

Pushing on up the stairs, Julie looked exhausted and Peter offered to carry her bag, which she was thankful for. They made excellent progress and eventually, the lights to the exit shone ahead of them. Peter had regained his strength and felt positively rejuvenated, his energy levels at a high. Perhaps the fleece had given him something else other than his life back.

As soon as they appeared, Hermes motioned to them to be quiet until they were outside.

Both followed him, no one saying anything for about two minutes.

Hermes spoke with excitement in his voice, 'By the gods, you did it.'

'I didn't, Julie did. She was incredible; got the chalice, filled it, then we were attacked, and…' Peter could not control his excitement as they almost began running down the hill.

'Attacked by whom?'

'The one who has been following us all this time.'

Julie said nothing, she just kept walking.

'He shot me, twice. I was dead, but she brought me back by using the fleece.'

'You were shot… and she used the Golden Fleece?'

'Twice, but she killed the guy.'

'How?'

Julie said matter-of-fact though her eyes glowed. 'I used the Gorgon's head. And in my anger for what he had done, as I am sure he's the one who killed Alexis, I picked up a sword and smashed him to bits. After, I picked up the fleece, put it over Peter, and prayed. As you can tell, it worked.'

'By the gods of Olympus, Julie, that is amazing.'

'I guess it is, as I still can't believe it either,' then noncha-lantly, she asked. 'How far did you park?'

'Nearly there.' All three descended rapidly the last part and made their way to the car.

Peter opened the door, waited for Julie to dive into the back seat, and followed. Julie put her arms around him.

Hermes climbed in, checked the rear-view mirror, smiled, and started the engine.

Back at the house, the first thing he did was call his Father.

Aphrodite sat on a chair at the table. She did not speak, but on her face was the look of admiration. True, this human was still her enemy, but she could not help but feel a sense of pride for her being able to beat the odds and prove her wrong. The sense of jubilation in the house was clear, as gods and mortals drank together.

'My Father wants to speak with you.' Hermes handed the phone across to Julie.

She took the call outside. The night air was warmer than expected, and she stood with just her T-shirt on.

'Mrs Cole, Hermes told me what happened. You are a remarkable woman, incredible, really. Knowing Hades as I do, I suspected he must have sent one of his ruthless killers. Now, I am also sure he is the one who killed poor Alexis. But you… you stopped him from hurting anyone else. Your story is as good as any of the stories told in the Odysseys of old. You are an amazing woman, Julie. Did you use perfect thought?'

'Thank you for your kind words but I just did what had to be done.' She found it difficult to speak, the emotions of the night fast catching up with her.

'Tomorrow…' Zeus paused. 'Tomorrow, you begin the most perilous part of the journey. You will travel to the Underworld, where you will need all the courage you have shown today and the fighting spirit I know lives within you. There is a saying that a famous Englishman once used to describe Greek heroism. If I remember correctly, it says, *Until now we used to say that the Greeks fight like heroes. Now we shall say: The heroes fight like Greeks.* You, Julie, are that heroine.'

'Well, I'm not Greek, I'm American, but I appreciate the sentiment.' Julie sensed he was smiling at her comment.

'Greek or American, Mrs Cole, you are one remarkable

woman. I pray that the next part of your odyssey will reunite you with Richard and that you will both come out safely.'

'Thank you, Mr Christoulides.' She still couldn't call him Zeus. Even after all she had been through, there was always a feeling of incredulity about this entire journey, one that with every step she took brought her closer to Richard.

'Safe Travels, Mrs Cole.' He closed his phone.

Julie walked back into the house. Some food had been prepared, and all four sat at the table.

'You impressed my Father then?' Aphrodite's tone was just a little condescending.

'It would appear so.' Julie's answer was matter-of-fact.

'Let's hope you impress me tomorrow when we go into the Underworld.' Aphrodite snatched a piece of bread and pulled it apart.

The comment only amplified the gravity of the task ahead.

'Let's forget about tomorrow and celebrate tonight.' Hermes was keen to cut the air of foreboding that was circulating around the table. 'More wine, more beer, and lots of food. Let's get this party started.' He began pouring drinks into glasses and a celebration began.

By the time they had all consumed their fill, what was left on the table was more empty wine and beer bottles and a selection of uneaten food.

Peter was first to rise from the table. 'That's me for the night. Thank you, one and all.' He kissed Julie on the cheek and made his way up the spiral staircase.

'I shall leave as well.' Aphrodite stood up. 'I will see you tomorrow.'

Hermes kissed her on the forehead and opened the door. She walked out and was gone into the midnight moonlight.

'Thank you, Hermes, we could not have done this without you.'

'I have known many brave men and a few women too, but

they have been gods or demi-gods. I have never known a mortal with courage such as yours. The love you carry for your husband is something that all of us, gods and mortals should aspire to. I am glad I got to know you, Julie Cole. Thank you.'

Unable to formulate a reply, Julie took his hand and held it. 'I'm glad I met you too.' She moved toward the stairs before turning to him one last time. 'Goodnight.' Then she walked up the stairs and along the passageway to her bedroom. Closing the door behind her, she plopped herself on the bed, cradled the pillow, and cried herself to sleep.

19

THE PLAN

'Today will be like no other you will experience as mortals.' Hermes spoke as they sat drinking their breakfast coffee. 'What you are about to do, see, and hear will test you to where you will believe your sanity has left you. This is something no one can prepare you for, not even my Father, so I suggest you spend the daylight hours learning all you can about the Underworld. I wish I could tell you more, but I can't, because the realm of the dead is beyond your understanding. You must experience it for yourself.'

'If I wasn't scared before, I am now.' Peter remarked.

'No, Peter, you will not be scared, you will be terrified. What lies ahead for both of you is something that cannot be explained. All I can do is get you to the entrance. From there, Aphrodite will join you. After that, you are on your own.'

'Where is the entrance?' Julie queried.

'On the other side of the Island. Many people think they know where it is and there are countless stories of many who went searching for it… Well, they are now considered missing, as they never returned. I can tell you this, none of those tales are true, just made-up nonsense to excite the tourists who want to be scared. I know because I am the only one here on the island who knows where the actual entrance is. Hence why only I can take you there.' His voice and countenance changed, no longer looking like the jovial host of last night. There was a new persona, one that the two mortals had not met or heard before; angst filled his words, too aware of the perils that awaited them all. 'I have some drawings here, which you need to memorize because you cannot take anything into the Underworld that has not been sanctified. Your chalice was given to you by Zeus, the eye too, so that is fine, everything else you leave behind. Do you understand?' Hermes insisted.

Peter took the folded maps, opening them on the table. As he moved his finger over the diagram he appreciated the sheer scale of the place. Each section was painted in a different colour and the text was all in ancient Greek.

Hermes looked across the table at Julie. 'Do you see what I mean?'

'No, I'm sorry I don't.'

'I told you I would tell you about the one mortal who went to the Underworld. Do you know the story of Orpheus?'

'No.' Julie looked puzzle as if she should know.

'Perhaps you might recognise this.' Hermes moved over to a small table upon which was an old-style record player. He opened a drawer and took from it a long-playing record, placed it on the turntable, and switching it on.

The music started slowly; it was the overture to Orpheus in the Underworld. The music drifted between them, no one said anything, it was the perfect way to set the scene for what was about to come.

'Orpheus was our greatest musician, perhaps the greatest of all times, blessed by his father Apollo who gave him instructions on the art of music, and presented him with a Golden Lyre with strings taken from his own hair. Orpheus's voice, like his prowess in playing was unsurpassed, it was almost hypnotic, as he used this talent to… as you say, *Charm the birds from the trees*. Apart from his music, Orpheus had one other passion, he was in love with Eurydice. She captivated his heart, his songs of love for her were heard all over the kingdom, even by the Gods in Olympus.

'When Orpheus played, all was right in the world. So, it was no surprise that soon this doting couple would marry. But instead of living happily ever after as your stories say, there was a harbinger of doom that hung over them, just waiting for the right moment to crush their happiness. This happened one day when Eurydice whilst walking, caught the eye of Aristaeus, a minor god of country comforts. His lust for her becoming evident as he followed her home. As he began to catch up, she called to Orpheus who lay strumming on his lyre. Hearing her distress, he came running to rescue her. In her need to escape, she ran faster and faster, dropping all the things in her basket and caught her foot on a stone which sent her tumbling. Her fall into a dry ditch disturbed a sleeping viper who struck without thought and bit into her ankle. Orpheus dropped into the ditch but it was too late, the snake had done its business. It is said that his screams cracked rocks and fissures and the earth opened. But to no avail, his beloved was gone.

'Now we get to the part that affects you. Lost in grief, Orpheus stopped playing. This had a residual effect as the people and those around him lost their harmony, discourse broke out throughout the kingdom, even Olympus felt oddly strange and empty. Apollo had watched his son suffer for almost twelve months, his grief beyond comprehension, affecting all around him, and could take no more.'

'How does this affect us?' Julie queried.

'I am coming to that…' Hermes smiled. 'Seeing his son's unending grief, Apollo came to him with a plan. He told him, "You must go and bring her back, because if anyone can do it, you can. Your music will be your guide." He gave Orpheus back his lyre and new golden strings from his hair, and that's when they called me. As the purveyor of souls, I could go into the Underworld but not with a mortal, see the connection now? Orpheus had a good idea what lay ahead but just in case, I gave him this map.'

'He went to the Underworld, and he was mortal?' Julie said.

'Yes. His first challenge was Charon, the Ferryman. Orpheus began playing his music as the boat approached and the chambers normally devoid of atmosphere, started to resonate with the tunes that escaped from the Lyre. Charon pulled up close as if in a trance and waved the mortal aboard. He didn't even take his payment, so enthralled was he by the sounds. People say that if he could smile he would have, at such an exquisite break from his normal routine.

'Orpheus left the boat to step literally into the jaws of Hades' pet, the three headed hellhound Kerberos. He played a tune that made the hound's ears twitch, six ears all moving in harmony as the strands of music vibrated through the darkness. The hound stretched out across the floor then rolled onto its back kicking wildly, as if the music had penetrated his skin, and within a few seconds was asleep. As Orpheus continued further and deeper into the labyrinths of the dead, he encountered phantoms and monsters, who were all bewitched by his music. Upon entering a large chamber, he was confronted by the three judges of the Underworld, Minos, Aeacus, and Rhadamanthus who saw the disturbance as punishable by death.

'Orpheus ignored their words and began to strum on his lyre. The judges and those in the chamber had never heard such sounds. The music penetrated the blackness of their souls, each note more beautiful than the last. As Orpheus sang, his voice opened chasms in the darkness and for the first time in centuries, light penetrated the chamber. He had created just the impression he needed and the trigger for the Lord of the Dead to appear. As

Hades entered the accompanied by his wife Persephone, the music stopped.

'Hades approached Orpheus with one thing in mind, his destruction. But before Hades could speak, Orpheus began a song so soulful and full of emotion that Hades stopped and with Persephone beside him, sat to listen. Orpheus was conquering the Underworld, note by note. As he came to the end of his piece, the Lord of the Dead had mellowed so much that he moved towards Orpheus and spoke to him.

'Why are you here mortal? It is death to enter the Under-world, to trespass upon my hallowed grounds, yet you risk this to come here? Why?'

'Orpheus seized his chance and continued to play, *'My wife is here and I need her back, I can't live without her. She was taken from me. Her name is Eurydice, I must have her back.'*

'You must have her back? no one here demands anything, except me.'

'Orpheus increased the tempo and the volume of his music; it was becoming hypnotic. Persephone stepped forward and whispered into Hades' ear and within seconds Eurydice stood before Orpheus. Their kiss and embrace is said to have melted some of the wickedness of the chamber, love had penetrated the darkness, it was a feeling even Hades could not ignore.

'Play one more tune and you will be reunited with your wife.' Hades said.

'It was not a command, merely a request. Both Hades and Persephone sat, as did those in the chamber, all becoming more engrossed in the new atmosphere. The strains of the music filtered through the walls and the floors, the notes themselves having a life of their own, each one penetrating the soul of the dead. As Orpheus built to a crescendo, Hades realised what he was about to do, give back a soul. This was not in his nature but his word was his bond, so he needed a way to perhaps maintain his reputation without being considered a fool.

'You may leave now but under one condition. As you travel back to the sunlight, your wife will remain ten paces behind you. Should you look back at her at any time, she will return to me.'

'Orpheus, confident he had won her back, looked towards Hades, smiled, and gave a last triumphant strum on his lyre. *'That won't happen.'*

'He began the journey back, his wife following. As he climbed more and more, he kept calling to her, making sure she was still behind him. When sunlight began to appear ahead, he knew he had barely ten feet to go, but just before they got to the exit, confident she was right behind him, Orpheus turned... Eurydice was lost to him, sent back to the Underworld, and he was banned from ever going there again.'

'That is a sad story.' Julie muttered.

Also enthralled by the story, Peter said. 'This reminds me of the Old Testament story of Lot and Sodom and Gomorrah. When God told Lot's wife not to look back at the destroyed twin cities. But she did, and was turned into a pillar of salt.'

Hermes turned to Julie. 'You must always have faith in the one who follows you. One moment of doubt and they too could be lost forever.'

Julie took the map and spread it out across the table.

'This is all that is left of Orpheus' journey.' Hermes tapped the ancient parchment in front of them, 'Follow my finger,' he traced and began pointing to places. 'This is Tartarus, the domain of the Titans. When my Father defeated them, he cast them in there. It is a dank, dark, and dreadful place. No light shines there, the sun can never penetrate its blackness. It is a terrifying place, where evil lives and proliferates. Avoid this place.'

Peter moved closer to the map.

Hermes nodded satisfaction, his captive audience of two was intensely concentrated on his every word. 'Tartarus is not part of the Underworld, so, if you take a wrong turn, get out of there fast. Richard is more likely to be in one of two places. Either at the Asphodel Meadows, a place for ordinary people, those who have done no wrongdoing, but neither have they achieved a status in life. Ordinary people who led ordinary lives go here. The second choice will be the Mourning Fields. This is a sad place, where the souls of those whose love was unrequited dwell, mourning their loss. But I suspect Richard won't be there.

'Then we come to Elysium, probably the best place in the Underworld. Heroes are taken here. This is where the likes of Achilles and Hector reside. Demigods and heroes, even some distinguished men of letters you will find there, but I fear, not Richard. Finally, there are the Isles of the Blessed. After a soul reaches Elysium, he or she has a choice, to stay or be reborn. If a soul is reincarnated three times and reaches Elysium the same number of times it is then exalted and sent to the Isles of the Blessed to live for eternity in serenity and peace. Richard has not done this yet so he will not be there.'

Both Julie and Peter studied the map. Their fingers moving over the surface, pointing out the different areas of interest.

'No one can be sure where he is presently, except perhaps Persephone. But you will only find that out once you reach her. Until then, it is all guesswork. Study the map, because one wrong turn and you could find yourself stuck in the Underworld forever.'

The warning was clear. Hermes was laying it all on the line, but it was their decision which path to follow. Not even Aphrodite could help them if they deviated from the plan, they would be on their own.

'Okay, good, you have the map. Now, we must look at what you are likely to face when you get to the Underworld, or even before you get there. I will take you by boat to the cave. Once inside, Aphrodite will join you, and the three of you will then row slowly through the cave. At some point, as you get closer to the entrance, the light will fade and a thick mist will appear. It's a black mist and you cannot see ahead of you. By then the boat will have changed into Charon's Ferry. Do not turn around to see the Ferryman take the coin my Father gave you, just toss it to the back of the boat. He will collect it and steer you towards your destination, which will be the gates. Once they are open, Charon will row you towards the entrances. Remember what I told you, there are five, one for each domain. You must choose which one to take.'

'How will I know?' There was real angst in Julie's question.

'You won't until you get there and then you must use *perfect thought* for the answer.'

'Now, I feel sick… I need some water.' She stood up, walked across to the tap, turned it on, grabbed a glass, filled it, and gulped down the cold liquid.

Peter and Hermes watched as the colour returned to her pale face.

'Are you okay?' Peter took her hand and squeezed it.

'Thank you, yes. But I am worried and scared of what might happen to us.'

'You wouldn't be human if you weren't,' Hermes said. 'So far, this odyssey has tested you as a mortal, but now you are entering the world of the gods. All that has gone before is the prelude to what lies ahead. You must keep the courage you had in Zeus' cave. Keep it tight inside you because you're going to need it. You will both need it when you come face to face with Hades, as you surely will.'

'I thought we could sneak in and get out without him knowing.' Peter suggested.

Hermes smiled then laughed aloud but his next words delivered a message of foreboding. 'He knows everything. He knows you are coming, just not when! So surprise is the one thing on your side.'

'At least we have that, I hope.' Peter added curtly.

'Spend the rest of the day relaxing and looking over the map.

I am going to find Aphrodite and tell her what the plans are.' Hermes got up and walked to the door.

'I am frightened, Peter,' Julie looked into his eyes.

He squeezed her hand tighter. 'I am scared enough for both of us.'

~

HERMES HAD WAITED for half an hour for Aphrodite to show. The rendezvous was at a quiet spot high in the mountains, surrounded by trees and a small waterfall which brought fresh water down from the rocks. The sun was warm, and he lit a cigarette. The smoke from it billowed into the air.

'Smoking, Hermes? I thought you had given up. Father will not be pleased. Nervous, are we?' Aphrodite stood by the rocks, throwing tiny pebbles into the water.

'I'm not, but you should be, as you have never been to the Underworld. Hades would love to keep you there, and taunt Father for all eternity if he captured you. You do realize this, don't you?'

'I know. But if I can get Adonis back, I will take my chances with Hades.'

'He will not bargain with you; he will just imprison you to keep as his pet.'

'I'm sure he'll try, but he won't succeed, Persephone will not allow it. Besides, when I return with Adonis, all the gods will know and we can then take our place together in Olympus. We deserve that honour.'

'My sister, what if it's not Adonis who is freed but the mortal? What will you do then?'

'That will not happen. Adonis will show his true self and we will be united for all time.'

'Be careful, Aphrodite, these mortals have an inner strength I have not seen before. And she is remarkable in the way she has focused herself on this task. Never have I seen a woman with such tenacity, such passion, and belief. Julie is the one you must conquer, not Hades.'

'If it comes to it, I will take care of her and her ungrateful husband.'

'It is true what they say, hell hath no fury like a woman scorned, or a goddess. And that, my dearest sister, is exactly where you will be walking into, Hell.'

As Aphrodite walked away, she turned and answered. 'You get me there, and I will look after myself.'

Hermes threw two large stones into the pool and watched the water ripple towards the bank. 'I pray you do, sister.' His words were for his ears only.

20

IN ALL HIS GLORY

When Hermes arrived back at the house, he realised he now had things he needed to tell and warn Julie and Peter about. Naturally, the most pressing was that Aphrodite was going to be a problem. She was hell-bent on ensuring Adonis returned with her, not Richard returning to Julie. Entering the room, he saw both asleep in each other's arms on the small sofa.

As if sensing someone had entered the house, Peter opened his eyes, smiled, and uncoiled himself from Julie. 'Sorry we crashed out, she is exhausted.' He said, embarrassed.

'No problem. Did you find out any more about where you are going?'

'Yes, I read some of these books… the ones in English. But you never mentioned what lies inside the gates.'

'Like a good host, I saved the best for later.' Hermes gave him a slight grin. 'I did not want to worry you anymore than you are already. I was going to tell you once you were on the boat, but no matter, I will do so when she wakes up.'

'I am awake, just closed my eyes. I am too nervous to sleep.' Julie sat up.

'Good. But before I tell you what to expect, I must tell you to beware of Aphrodite. She has put it in her mind that she will return with Adonis and not you with Richard. She is my sister, but I believe she is wrong. No one knows who or what spirit lives in Richard until you awaken him. So, be wary of whatever plan she has in mind, you have come too far to be cheated.'

'Thanks for the warning, Hermes. But I have dealt with her before, so I know what to expect… well, at least I think I do.' Julie rose from the sofa and went to sit at the table. 'You were going to explain what else we should know and what lies inside the gates?'

'Yes. When the gates open, you will hear Sirens' voices, who will call to you to take the path towards them. That route leads to Tartarus, so use the eye to protect you. Once you are at the entrance to the Underworld, you will find the emotions of Grief, Anxiety, Diseases, and Old Age. Fear, Hunger, Death, Agony, and Sleep also live there, together with Guilty Joys. Opposite them and close to the entrance doors is War and a plethora of beasts, like Centaurs, Gorgons, the Lernaean Hydra, Chimera, and Harpies, whom you have seen before. But perhaps the most significant of all these phenomena is in the middle of the island, for there stands an Elm Tree, where false dreams cling to every leaf.'

'That sounds daunting.' Peter didn't know what else to say.

'I will prepare you as best as I can. Now, ah… I have something for you. Julie, where is the chalice with the Gorgon's blood?'

'I keep it in my room, I will fetch it.'

'Please.' Hermes moved away from the table and opened a cupboard that stood at the back of the room.

Julie came down the stairs carrying the chalice.

'Thank you, leave it on the table.' Hermes had two boxes in his hands. 'Take these upstairs, open them, put them on, then come back down.'

Peter followed Julie upstairs, each carrying their own box.

Inside their rooms, they opened the boxes and saw a note lying on tissue paper. 'Remove all of your clothes and things that come from your time and wear this.'

Peter placed the note on the bed then returned his attention to the contents; a Cretan tunic and a pair of sandals. Stripping naked, he held the tunic up in front of him. 'You've got to be joking.' He mumbled as he nonetheless put on the ancient clothing.

Next door, Julie was repeating the exercise, only her robes were more intricate. She stood naked looking in the mirror, all trappings of her modern life vanishing before her. The only thing remaining, the blue-eye that hung around her neck.

She picked up the shimmering white Chiton designed in natural pleats, its emphasis placed on the bosom, where it gathered in a double fold, designed to expose some flesh. She put the dress on, it hung down to her sandals. Her hair needed pinning or a clip to keep it up, so her shoulders were bare and her neckline prominent. The fabric folds were crisp and sharp, and when she moved her sandaled feet peeped slightly from beneath the hem. Gazing at her own image, she felt like a goddess. She made her way down the spiral stairs.

She knew she looked good, but the reception she got was still unexpected.

Standing in the middle of the room, dressed in a white tunic that covered his body, except for his bare shoulders, Peter stared at the vision of loveliness that she presented. A smile of appreciation spread all over his face. 'You look wonderful.'

Her eyes lit up.

'Mrs Cole, you look like a goddess. Permit me one minor alteration.' Hermes moved across to the cupboard, took out a small box, opened it, then moved across to Julie. In his hand, he held an intricate coloured hair piece complete with a gold band edged with small golden leaves. He placed it on her head and removed the pins she had used earlier. 'Perfect.' He said, pleased with his work.

All three stared at each other. It was odd, the two mortals looked like gods and the god looked mortal. The irony was not lost on them.

'I suppose it is my turn.' Hermes turned around, stripped naked, then as he turned to face them again, his transformation took place.

Peter and Julie stood mesmerised, for standing before them was a god of Olympus. His countenance had changed, because although he still looked young, his beard was white, fully grown, and his face had become brilliantly tanned, as were his bare arms and legs. His upper body was covered with a golden breastplate and in his hand, he carried a staff which was twisted into two serpents. A broad-brimmed hat with two small decorative wings on either side sat on his head, and looped leather supported his sandals up to his knees and two small wings protruded from his ankles.

Peter had only ever seen them in their tattoo form, but now he was seeing them for real. Hermes was magnificent.

His voice carried an echo as he spoke, 'Mortals, this is the true Hermes, Messenger to the gods and Purveyor of Souls. I greet you as a god.'

Julie and Peter were in awe of the being standing before them. Not even Zeus, the king of the gods, had been as impressive in his deity as Hermes was. Not sure whether to curtsey or bow, the two fell to their knees in homage and wonder, even closing their eyes. When they opened them again, Hermes was back in his modern-day dress. It might have been mere seconds, but he had to be one of the fastest change artists ever.

'So now you know for sure I am who I say I am. I hope I didn't scare you.'

Both got up, and the room became full of superlatives as each one poured compliment after compliment at Hermes.

'When this is all over, I am going to write a book.' Peter grinned at Julie.

'No one will ever believe you.' She laughed, it took her feelings of tension away.

'Okay, now, I have one more thing to tell you.' Hermes looked at them. 'And after that, I suggest you get some more sleep.'

'I don't know about you,' Julie glanced at Peter, 'but I've had enough sleep for one day.'

He nodded, 'Me too.'

'Fine.' Hermes said. 'Then please pass me the Gorgon's blood.'

Julie reached over and took the chalice from the table.

Hermes walked across to the small cupboard and took out a small jug. 'When you enter the Underworld, the creatures there will take you as being dead. If you went as you are, you would not get through the gates, so you must be dead. Or at least look like you are. In here is a potion, or elixir, for the dead. I will pour some into the right-hand side,' he tipped the jug and decanted the thick liquid. 'Remember, there are now two sides, blood on the left, and potion on the right. You must sip twice, no more. Sip more and you will be dead. But don't do it until Charon has boarded, and the boat is moving towards the gates. A green or grey aura will then circulate around your body, giving the impression that your soul is in transit. You will stay like this all the time you are in the Underworld, only after you leave will the aura disappear. So, do you understand? Only two sips.'

Both looked worried, their faces frowning in unison.

Seeing their anxiety, Hermes tried to placate them. 'You will be fine. I am told it tastes disgusting so two sips are all you need. Oh, yes, I told you about the Sirens and how they will try to steer you towards them, as they did with Odysseus. He was tied to his ship's mast so he could hear their voices, but his crew had wax in their ears so they could not. Well, nothing so crude for the two of you. The clothes you have on also boast hoods, so put them on after you take the potion to blot out the Sirens' voices. Once you are past them, you can remove them. Do you have any questions?'

Peter stood up to look Hermes in the eye. 'If all goes well, as we hope it will, how do we get out of there?'

'I thought you would ask that, eventually, but that is not my domain. The one who knows the way is Persephone. She has the knowledge of how to get through the labyrinth that leads to the exit of the Underworld, or to give it its proper name, Hades. Yes, the god and the place have the same name. I bet you didn't know that from your history books.'

'Aren't you full of surprises.' Julie smiled and winked at him.

Hermes glanced at his watch. 'It will soon be time. We will take the car after sunset and drive to the boat, and from there we row to the entrance. This part of the island is quiet, few fishermen or boats travel here. You can't see the entrance from the water, as it is hidden in the rocks that surround the side of the cliffs. We will be alone until then, and Aphrodite will join you once you are in the cave. Now, you know as much as I do, and that you must use *perfect thought* to get you through this.' He looked straight at Julie. 'Remember, courage does not come from a badge or medal, it comes from your heart and soul. It is not something you wear, it lives in you. I see it in both of you and that is why you will be successful; and I pray that you are.'

'Hermes, you have shown us your true divinity, and your human side, we cannot express how much you mean to both of us. I wish that one day we will meet again, whether in your world, or ours. Thank you.' Julie's words were heartfelt.

Sensing the emotions building inside her, Hermes took her hand and kissed her on the forehead. No one said anything, they all just sat back at the table.

Then Peter suggested. 'Let's look at that map one last time.'

21

CHARON THE FERRYMAN

The sun had set, all was prepared; two mortals and a god, driving to an unknown future. No one spoke. Julie sat looking out of one window and Peter the other. The roads were quiet as they drove up and down the winding cliffs, the lights from passing cars their only sign of civilisation. There were no villages or towns, just a distant street lamp that flickered on and off. A group of feral cats sat by the roadside watching the car as it disappeared around corners.

As they came to a crest on the side of the mountain road, they had a splendid view of the moon. It was grey and full but beginning to show signs of red creeping across its surface; the blood moon had begun to turn. Time was against them.

The car began heading down the mountainside, picking up speed as it took each bend with care. The sound of crashing waves against an unseen shore reached them, but as they entered the beach road they skirted along, white-crested plumes meandered rhythmically towards the rocks.

Hermes stopped the car and motioned to his passengers to get out while he walked towards a rowboat anchored nearby. He pushed it into the water, released the rope that braced it, then climbed in and picked up the oars.

Peter guided Julie on board as the waves flushed against the side of the small vessel.

'We will row for about a hundred metres then pull into the side before the entrance, and that is where I leave you. Once inside, the cave's water will be turquoise, but there are small lanterns hanging on the wall, so you will see for a while. Only when the clouds form and the darkness looms will the boat change and Charon will board. Peter, do you know how to row?'

'Yes, I did some rowing in the forces. And when I lived in Pissouri, I went night fishing regularly.'

'Excellent.' Hermes began rowing faster. His arm muscles pulled at the oars powerfully, building up good momentum as the craft moved swiftly through the waves, leaving small whirlpools in their wake.

Julie stared towards the shore while clutching the chalice in her hands, the instructions she had to follow secure in her mind.

Hermes slowed the boat, pulling it forward towards the rocks. 'We are here and this is where I leave you. There is no more to be said, you know what to do.'

Peter and Julie watched the rocks as the boat drifted towards an opening almost invisible from where they sat.

Turning to the departing god, she asked. 'Where are you going now?'

'I think I've had enough of this mortal life for a while, so I am going back to Olympus to party.' He stood up in the boat and his transformation began again; no longer the cool dude, but his other self, Hermes, Greek god. The wings on his ankles fluttered, and he hovered just above the water, then within seconds he was in the air.

Both mortals turned to see him fly, but he had already disappeared from sight. For the first time in a while, they felt alone. Peter automatically moved closer to Julie and taking up the oars, began to row. Manoeuvring inside the opening, they saw it was as Hermes had said; the water reflecting a brilliant turquoise colour. With care, Peter navigated the slender corridors of rock.

Slowly, the oars moved back and forth, pushing the boat forward. All was quiet inside, the only sound that of the creaking oars dipping into the water. Looking around and behind them, Julie sensed they were getting close, as the water was getting darker, and the turquoise changing into deep blue. Small patches of black clouds appeared, and it was then the boat rocked sideways.

Julie turned to see Aphrodite sitting behind her.

'Did you miss me?' Aphrodite's first words were tinged with sarcasm.

'I wondered when you'd show up, almost thought you were going to miss the party.' Julie's response was equally sarcastic.

'Ladies, please, no bickering. If we are going to get this done, we must all work as a team.' Peter's remonstrations were cut short.

As the clouds thickened, a deep sense of fear circulated around the boat and it was then it cracked and swelled. Peter dropped the oars and clung to Julie, whereas Aphrodite gripped the sides as it rocked vigorously. Wooden slats splintered, water poured in, and all three tried to hang on. The boat rose higher in the water then stopped, its shape distorted, the wood blistered, and within seconds it was covered in a green slime that slithered down its edge.

Looking down the side of the boat they could tell it had stretched between fifteen to twenty feet, and aged about two hundred years or more, and there was a distinct smell emanating from the rear. Charon had boarded and was using a pole to steer the vessel.

Julie reached into a small pocket on her dress, pulled out the coin, and tossed it to the back of the boat.

Charon grunted loudly as he caught it with his skeletal hand.

Aphrodite was about to turn to see where the coin had landed when she remembered she was not supposed to. She felt Julie's grip on her hand. Clearly, the mortal had been told likewise because she still said,

'Don't.'

She let go of the mortal's hand and sat back.

Julie opened the chalice and passed it to Peter.

Taking it, he lifted it to his mouth and sipped twice. He almost spat it right out. It was so foul, the taste a nauseating blend of stale bread and who knew what else. His eyes watered.

Julie tasted the elixir. It was putrid, reminding her of the smell of a dead dog she had once found in her Boston backyard as a child. She too felt her eyes water.

Looking at Peter, she noticed his body had become a shroud of death, a translucent green glow emanating around him. She glanced down at her own hands. They too were like Peter's, as was her entire body. Even Aphrodite had become enshrouded in the green aura. All three were prepared for the Underworld. The clouds turned black and moved towards them.

22

THE ODYSSEY: PART THREE

s the boat poked its way through the mist, there was little or no movement as the ferryman eased his way through the murky waters. His passengers sat passively reliant upon the skills of the boatman to get them through safely. In the distance, haunting voices drifted as echoes in the haze, which began to evaporate, making the walls visible. As they sat in the confines of their self-imposed prison, the very walls swayed back and forth, giving off a fluid appearance, and vivid colours —this, the result of a leaking mass of serpents that began escaping from their rock sanctuary.

At first, the wall's colour was predominantly green, but as more serpents dropped from the crevices to the floor, patterns began to mix, as bodies coiled and slithered across the surface. There was no distinct design to the gathering, just a huddled mass of writhing bodies in tandem with the collective hissing sound emanating from their mouths; their long fangs exposed and their testing tongues teasing the fetid air. More dribbled from the wall, among them a large, thickly-coiled serpent whose markings were unremarkable, but from its sheer size alone it was clear this was the most respected of all.

As it made its way through the piles of brethren gathered at the water's edge, it looked straight across at the boat. Its eyes focused upon the vessel, the tongue flipping in and out of its mouth as its body slipped slowly into the water. It coiled and twisted, gaining speed as it came ever closer to the boat's side. When within striking distance, Charon pulled his heavy oar from the water and hit it with such force it ricocheted off the bank, its body broken and bloodied. This was the chance the rest had been waiting for; they pounced upon the crippled body and began to devour the flesh. The unexpected and unlikely meal was also key for more inhabitants of the caves to dine on what was left of the carcass. Charon ploughed on.

He had stirred his oar no more than five times when from the side of the great river bank, a figure moved forward; it was menacing, ominous, and cast no reflection. In the half-light, it was clear that it was a large man, with great, wide shoulders and looked taller than the others within the surrounding area.

Charon's Ferry came to a halt, the waves lapping the sides as the figure moved from his seated position to stand and survey the boat and its inhabitants. There had been several moments of fear on this journey but presently, this was turning into the scariest. The stillness of the water, fading light, and the approaching figure all added to the dimension of dread running through them. The sheer malevolence of the figure owed much to the atmosphere and it was all too clear when Aphrodite whispered,

'The god of Death himself.'

Thanatos moved across the water, his body two to three feet above the waves, his glide perfected to skim the surface where the boat drifted. His movement so concise and defined that it brought him quickly alongside the shrouded figures. He leaned in, to sniff at the newly transported sprits. The familiar smell of death they had consumed greeted his senses and he seemed satisfied that the passengers were indeed on their way to the Underworld. Death retired to its former position and retook its place.

Charon moved the boat forward.

SLOWLY, the boat pushed through the black mists again. There was no mistaking this water, it was the River Styx. How Charon navigated into this channel they did not know, but as they moved ever onward, voices broke the silence and loud screaming echoed across the walls. Sounds of crying and loud sobbing mingled with other noises, creating a cacophony of agony and sadness that resonated and bounced against the rocks.

The boat turned in the river, and more voices spoke. First in whispers before becoming louder; the words incoherent, mere noises, then silence. The vessel slowed, then stopped, bobbing on an inky darkness. There was an eerie stillness, as all the other voices stopped. Nothing. The only sound coming from the gentle rocking on the calm, gloomy water. Not a whisper, or a word, just a deathly hush that ran through the occupants as they looked around for some sign of movement.

Then, a single voice came, so near one could almost touch it. It penetrated the minds of the listeners and was accompanied by several others so perfect in pitch and hypnotic they resonated around the walls, sending echoes in front and behind them. Realising these were the Sirens they had been warned about, Julie quickly threw the hood over her head, blotting out the sound. Peter followed suit as the voices grew louder, their lament soulful, enticing, and seductive.

The black fog lifted and they could see several semi-naked female Sirens stretched out, their hands beckoning invitingly, and displaying their bodies seductively. Oblivious to their attempts at temptation, the boat moved on, ignoring their pleas. The singing stopped.

Back to the almost dead silence, the only audible sound was the noise the Ferryman made as he pushed through the lapping black water. The boat jolted. Across from them, on the banks of the river, indistinct figures gathered. They looked like shadows, but each had their own characteristics.

Peter turned to get a better look, and as he did, a tremendous roar broke the silence.

A beast of awesome proportions and strangeness lurched towards the shoreline, its claws stretching to grab and maim, its mouth wide open as it belched out fire. Several creatures made up the Chimera. In front, it possessed the body of a lion and on its back was the head of a goat with a tail resembling a coiled snake.

As the wispy haze lifted, several other hideous-looking creatures lined up along the river's bank and turned their heads to eye them. One of the Harpies went as far as skirting the boat, then turned away screeching when it caught sight of Julie's bejewelled blue-eye around her neck. A distance away, one tree sat in the middle of the water.

The passageway's walls were covered in a green and purple slime that trickled down to the water's edge, the smell of decay so pungent it was difficult to keep the bile from leaving their throats, as they gagged on the stench.

As Charon dipped and pushed his pole one more time, the water bubbled, creating waves that rocked the boat to-and-fro and something moved beneath the disturbance.

Two huge circular wooden doors emerged and with them came the voices of Julie's nightmare, the one she had heard since childhood, 'Of course, of course, of course.'

Startled, Julie clasped Peter's hand tightly, her nails digging into his flesh. He felt nothing.

It was as if the voices were answering her question. She closed her eyes and visualised her dream, which was materialising before her. The gates were circular, resembling the large ball in her nightmare, and the boat was like the pin, able to pierce the gates. Somehow, she had created a premonition of this moment. She had always woken up before the pin passed through the balloon, now she was living it.

Once inside, the doors closed behind them and returned to the depths below, rocking the boat wildly, then as the waters of the Styx receded, the boat floated gently towards five separate channels. Charon stopped the boat, waiting to see which way his passengers were headed.

Taking the eye from around her neck and placing it in one hand, Julie moved to the front of the boat, held it over the bow, and waited. The eye glowed softly, then like a magnet, turned to the right.

Sinking his pole back in the water, Charon pushed down, nudging the boat towards the Elysian Fields.

23

THE FATES

*K*erberos, Hades' pet and guardian of the underworld, sat beside his master chomping at the thick metal chain attached to its neck. His wide mouth and snarling teeth, which worked almost independently from his three heads, competed against each other for the morsels of skin and bone that lay scattered about the floor. On the hound's back and rear-end were venomous snakes, twisting and cavorting, forming intricate patterns on the hound's body. At its rear, another serpent acted as the animal's tail.

As master moved, so did the reptiles' bodies writhe with the creature. Hades stroked its back, touching the snakes' skin then looked down at the hound as it pulled on the chain and said. 'Guard.'

The word was enough for the hound to stop its protestations and take its position as *Guardian to the Underworld.* As Hades moved away, the hound settled in, his eyes and body alert to the task.

Hades' next move would take him away from his domain, something he despised; apart from going to the mortal world, which he regarded as a treat. When away, he was always aware of potential pretenders to his Kingdom. As grim as it was, the ruler of the Underworld commanded substantial power, something he cherished, and whether his brother did things by design or deceit, it was his and his alone.

However, presently, he made his way towards the one place where his power and that of his brother's had no value. The Kingdom of Moirai, the home of *The Fates*. The three sisters dwelled on the island with the distinct purpose of determining the fate of those who came under their judgement. Mortal or god, all fell to their destiny. Clotho controlled the spindle on which the thread of life was woven. Lachesis was known as the *allotter* or *drawer of lots*, the one who measured the thread. And finally, the most dreaded of the three, Atropos, also known as the most merciless, whose sole task was to cut the thread of life with her shears, choosing the time and method of a person's death. This was the place, Hades believed, where he would find his answers.

As he arrived on the island, he quickly took the only path leading away from the shore, and followed it, increasing his pace as he climbed upward, eager to find the sanctuary of the Moirai. He had never been there, or met *The Fates*; perhaps because he held no power over them and wanted to have the upper hand in all things. *The Fates* were an enigma and a challenge to his power in the most subtle of ways, but to learn the answers to his questions, he had to bow to their wisdom and accept whatever he was told. Not even he could challenge destiny.

The entrance was not what he expected. The pathway was smooth, the area clean, neat, and small clusters of bushes lined the walkway that led to a recess in a steep cliff. He moved inside. The interior was brightly lit and strains of music drifted towards him from what sounded like a harp or a lyre.

Following the melodic strain, he walked along a pathway that led into a corridor made entirely of rock, going deeper into the cave. The music grew louder as he sauntered towards it, then stopped. Ahead of him were three dazzling visions of beauty attired in flowing white gowns, decorated in clusters of gems and trimmed with gold.

The first one, majestic in her appearance had shiny white hair folded in tresses around her neck and shoulders. Her face, a perfect white, had her bright eyes focussed on Hades.

She stood up, 'You do us honour, my Lord.' Lachesis, *the drawer of lots*, addressed him as she held in her hand a thin thread, which she twirled around in her fingers.

Her sister, Clotho, was another picture of loveliness wearing the same type of dress and jewellery except, her red hair was loose, covering her shoulders. She sidled up to her sister, passing her a spindle.

'I have come—'

'We know why you have come, my Lord. We know everything. It is our purpose to know.' The voice came from the third sister, Atropos, who stood to the side brandishing a pair of shears in her hand. She appeared older, more mature in looks and stature, and her dress was also not as flattering as the others. Her special feature was her eyes, which shone in a way that seemed to mirror the person they were looking at, as if she could see inside their soul. She held the power over life, for with one snip of her shears, she could end it. 'The answer to your question is yes. We will show you, my Lord.'

Hades waited.

'Sisters,' On Atropos' command, the other two joined hands and walked in a circle while their bodies swayed to the music. 'Come into the centre, Lord.'

A rhythmic trance ensued.

Hades stepped between the women, his body tight against them, and as their momentum increased, so the circle expanded. Where there were three, there were now six, then twelve, while they kept dancing around him. He watched, mesmerised. Their movements conjured a vision, accompanied by a voice whispering from the circle. It had come from one of them but which one he was not sure.

'The servant you sent to dispose of the mortal is dead. Disposed of… in a way that even we could not have predicted.'

'What do you mean?' Hades demanded.

'See for yourself.'

Hades watched as the events from Zeus' cave unfolded.

'The mortal used the Gorgon's head to turn him to stone. She then took up a sword and smashed the petrified figure into tiny pieces, scattering them across the floor.'

Lachesis confirmed the statement with a nod of her head.

'The Gorgon's head is lost, in a place no one will ever find.'

Clotho's words were not what Hades wanted to hear, because that meant his plans for the Gorgon's blood had now come to a dead-end. This mortal woman had destroyed them. She would pay his price, and his price was high.

'Be aware, Lord, this mortal is powerful. Perhaps not as much as you, but look how she wields the sword. No mortal man or woman can use that sword in this way. She holds power, and yes, she is a challenge, one that you should take heed of.'

'It is true what my sister says.'

The circle vanished, leaving just the three women standing next to Hades.

Atropos moved forward, and with her piercing eyes stared directly into his. 'This mortal not only has the power of *perfect thought* but she has the all-seeing eye. It is a weapon so powerful that she could create havoc in your Kingdom. She could bring about a division in the Underworld where the Elysian Heroes would rise to rebel against your rule. Tread carefully with this mortal, one wrong move and your haven will be infiltrated, perhaps for all time.'

Hades pondered over what he heard. Dracos was gone, the Gorgon's head was gone, and if he didn't act quickly, his entire Kingdom could be gone too. The answers he had gained were not what he expected, and for the first time in decades, he feared for himself. If his brother was behind this so-called coup it was beyond subtle, it was clandestine in its very approach. By using this mortal woman, Zeus could make the Underworld his own and banish Hades to Tartarus to be exiled with the Titans. 'Show me more.' His voice rose as he insisted on having more knowledge from the sisters.

'There is no more to show you,' Atropos rebuked him.

'You must show me more, you are the only ones who have the power to do this, show me.'

'Even if we wanted to, we can't, the eye is blocking our vision. All we can tell you is that we see them at the Elysian Fields, but we don't know where they go afterwards.'

'You must seek your answers elsewhere, we can't help you anymore.'

The music stopped, and with it the three sisters disappeared.

Hades stood alone, perplexed by the revelations. In the sanctuary of the Moirai, it came to him that perhaps there was one other place to go to find his answers.

24

THE ELYSIAN FIELDS

Nobody in the boat was sure why Charon turned to steer towards the island they were fast approaching. A disgruntled murmur came from him at the back, as if this was an unplanned departure from his itinerary. The three passengers grew more nervous as the boat plied its way to shore. Charon eased into a small inlet which offered some docking facility, and the three disembarked.

Julie held Peter's hand, a motion not missed by Aphrodite, who decided she might as well follow them.

They meandered up from the shoreline with trepidation as they did not understand why they were there or what awaited them. Ahead was a brightly coloured curtain of mist, vibrant, as if many rainbows had clustered together, its light intensifying the closer they got.

Peter moved in front of the other two; he had seen something like this before, so he was aware of what to do. He held his hand up to the centre of the cloud and pushed it through, before stepping in and disappearing.

Somewhat nervously, Julie followed. Aphrodite did likewise.

The sight that greeted them was one of wonder. For in a

place of death and depravity, this was a place of pure beauty. Before them lay endless acres of green grass and brilliant yellow cornfields, all blessed with radiant light, which seemed stronger than sunlight but had little or no heat emanating from it, yet it was comfortable to walk in. As far as the eye could see the land was bathed in this light and the creatures that inhabited it only enhanced the majesty of the landscape. Rich birdsong rang throughout. As for the woodland creatures of this idyllic domain, none paid attention to the strangers as they moved through them.

Aphrodite was the first to speak. 'There is only one place this can be.'

'Where?' Julie was mesmerised as she turned on her heels to take in the full vista of her surrounds.

'This is the Elysian Fields, The Home of Heroes. I wonder why we have come here.'

Aphrodite's last words were the very question Julie was asking herself.

Peter stood impassively, surveying the landscape. 'We need to find out. If Richard is here, we will find him.' He held Julie's hand tighter as they began their search.

They walked through the fields towards what looked like a new road and scanned the place for people or signs of life other than the ones on four legs.

'What do you know about this place?' Peter said, turning to Aphrodite.

'I know that whoever comes to this place, deserves to be here, and has earned the right to be recognised as heroes, their honour is unbounded, unchallenged, and just. I can see why Adonis would be here. He is a god.'

'And Richard?' Julie aimed the remark directly at Aphrodite.

'A mere mortal, he is of no importance in this place.'

'Since according to you they are one and the same person I can see why we shouldn't worry.' Julie said.

Peter could see where this was going and intervened quickly.

'Please, ladies, we are all anxious and determined to find Richard and Adonis but we can only do so if we work together.' He admonished then stared in shock at Julie. 'Huh… look at yourself.'

Julie looked at her arms, legs, and body, all were returning to their natural state. Peter too had lost the aura, and the same was true of Aphrodite. The three were becoming themselves again.

Julie spoke. 'The shroud is gone. Which means, we have lost our protection. Why is this happening?'

'We are in the presence of Heroes, who do not recognise death. They are immortal, do not need any trappings of the beyond, and are unaffected death. They are pure and unsullied. But we cannot worry about ourselves. For now, we must continue to look for them.' Aphrodite's words made sense and resonated with her companions as she took the lead.

Peter took Julie's hand again, and they followed behind the goddess.

As they traversed through the cornfield, the sky turned a vivid blue and streaks of light shone down upon their shadows, which elongated, stretching like arrows towards a road ahead of them. Their heading was clear, they followed their shadows.

Aphrodite led the way, moving with no effort at all, her body gliding along the narrow walkway, her hips twisting slowly on their own axis. Her movements were so practiced and defined that it was easy to see why men would die for this vision.

Peter moved closer to Julie. It was the best way to deflect his eyes from the goddess' flirtatious parade.

Julie smiled and the two followed without words until they came to a long avenue flanked by golden statues.

Aphrodite stopped at the entrance, then turned to them. 'This is Heroes Avenue, and we will walk down The Pathway of Homage. Here, the heroes of our days are revered for all time. They are all here, Heroes you mortals have only ever read about in books or seen in your moving pictures. But for me, they are what our world is all about. Courage, bravery, obedience, and valour, the true worth of a Hero.'

The first thing they saw as they began down the avenue was an immense golden statue. Shimmering in the artificial sun, it depicted two lions on their hind legs, rearing their muscular bodies and their heads held proudly upwards.

As they entered this gateway, Aphrodite pointed to the first statue. It was bronze and ornately fashioned to enhance the figure's features to the point of appearing alive. 'This is Achilles, isn't he magnificent?'

Julie stood looking up at the demi-god. 'He is so handsome. But how do you know it's him, there are no names on these statues?'

'These heroes don't need names attached to them, their deeds and legends are etched not just in stone or bronze but in history, testaments to an age when champions were revered for their worth. I see none of these qualities in the ones you call celebrities, your modern-day heroes. There is no virtue in them and no value to their fellow man.'

Peter nodded his approval at the passionately delivered statement.

They passed by Achilles and came upon a line of statues, each one a hero in their own right.

Aphrodite pointed them out as they made their way down the roadway. 'Paris, the one who slew Achilles. And here is Hector, whom Achilles killed first, all over the love for a woman.'

'Sounds familiar,' Peter commented, drawing a quick glance from his female companions.

'Jason.' Aphrodite pointed. 'I have a special love for him. He and his Argonauts were so brave in capturing the Golden Fleece, I am glad to see he has been given his rightful place here.'

Behind Jason, about twelve-feet deep, was a group of male statues, each one an Argonaut.

Aphrodite smiled, as if she had triggered a memory. 'Here is one you might recognise, the Boy King, many call him Alexander the Great, hero and conqueror. He died far too young.'

Peter moved forward. There were more and more heroes, some he recognised, some he didn't. He stopped at one particular statue, it was not like any of the others. He pointed at it. 'Who is this?'

'Ah, this is the infamous Bellerophon.'

Peter stood looking up at the plinth and the figure on it. 'It doesn't look finished, and the face has no eyes.'

'My Father saw to that.' Aphrodite elaborated to the intrigued couple. 'Bellerophon was a Prince, respected and admired by all who knew him. It was he who killed the Chimera, the creature you saw earlier. No simple task, even for a god. And that is where the problem lies, for Bellerophon wanted to be accepted as a god.

'Perhaps because his father was Poseidon, or perhaps it was just his persistent ambition that pushed him to challenge the Father of the Gods. He laid his claim when he rode Pegasus. Yes, he rode Pegasus to Olympus. This angered Zeus, who didn't like his impertinence and immediately set about taking the imposter to task. He released a gadfly against Pegasus, which bit hard into the nag's flesh, throwing Bellerophon into a wood crowded with thorn bushes.

'Normally, he would have been stone dead as it was a great fall, but Zeus had other plans. He wanted the pretender to suffer for his challenge to his authority, so he blinded him instead. Bellerophon lived like that into his old age, a recluse, unwanted by mortals or by the gods. In many ways, I see why he is here. He was a hero, but with flaws.'

Julie moved past the statue and onto one that was slightly apart from the others, one that appeared to be carved in granite, so defined were its features. She stood looking up at the male figure with its proud and resolute pose, displaying a distinctive shield and sword which was brandished in a striking down stance. She moved closer and touched the stone. It felt like silk on her fingers, the surface unblemished, polished, and perfect. 'Who is he?'

Aphrodite stood next to her. 'This is the hero of Thermopylae, King Leonidas of Sparta. If ever a man deserved to be recognised here, it is him. All Greece owes a debt to him and his Three Hundred.'

Peter was about to mention that he had seen the film, but thought it might be crass in the presence of actual distinguished heroes.

'Look there,' Aphrodite pointed to the group of armed warriors standing behind the leader. 'Here are the mighty Three Hundred, with their King.' There was immense pride upon her face as she gloried in the heroes of ancient Greece.

The three continued down the avenue, Aphrodite pointing out the vast number of effigies lining both sides of the pathway, naming them as they moved along. Names that echoed in the annals of myth and legend for the modern-day observer. Only here cherished for their deeds and heroism.

'This is Odysseus, the one who had a hand in defeating the Trojans, for it was he who created The Wooden Horse.' Aphrodite paused at the next row, and smiling, turned to Julie. 'There are heroes here who never raised a sword in anger. These are the Greeks who did more to create the world you live in today than any other. This is Hippocrates, *The Father of Medicine*. Next to him, Plato, whose brilliant mind is a testament to intellect, for it was he who schooled Aristotle. And here... ah, here, we have the man who made all of this possible in his writings with his stories. This is Homer, who created The Odyssey. His tales of Greek gods gave you mortals a vision of my world and that of my Father. All you know about us stems from him.'

Julie looked at all the figures then posed a question. 'Why are there no women here?'

The goddess smiled. 'You are right, there are many women worthy of the title Hero, or Heroine. But in our civilisation this was a privilege reserved for men only, regardless of what status a woman aspired to.' She turned to Julie. 'Perhaps if you succeed in your own odyssey, you will be given recognition and it could change people's perceptions of the value of a woman, even here.'

Peter wrinkled his brow; the first genuine compliment Aphrodite had paid Julie. Was there finally respect for this mortal and what she was doing, as she did not lack in courage.

Dismissing Aphrodite's comment, Julie spoke with some urgency. 'All this is remarkable but we are no closer to finding them. I think we need to move quicker.' As she stepped ahead of the other two, the path took a sharp left turn and went down an incline.

Going along the road, they heard crowds cheering and laughing. Loud applause rang out from the area where the noises emanated at their loudest and stopping, they caught sight of a magnificent amphitheatre carved into the mountainside. They climbed up the hill to get a better view of the spectacle below.

From their vantage point they were able to look down upon a large seated crowd, who cheered at participants dressed in fine armour and who appeared to be locked in combat. It was difficult to make out who was fighting as there were several pairs on the field, each vying for control over their opponent. Fanfares and trumpets sounded and the fighters left the arena to be replaced by a new set of combatants.

The audience comprised a plethora of different people, all elegantly dressed, sporting the finest clothing and jewellery. Many were holding court, discussing the fighters' tactics as they placed wagers on who would be the victor and take the spoils, whatever they were.

As they continued watching, Julie turned around and standing on the crest of the hill where they were, appeared a stunning-looking young woman.

Slowly and deftly, the woman approached them. 'You are strangers here, where did you come from?' The young woman was as curious about them as they were of her.

Aphrodite looked straight at the new visitor. 'Andromeda, do you not recognise me?'

'Aphrodite, by the gods!' Andromeda took a quick look at the strangers. 'Wait… you are the woman, the mortal they speak of. But… Aphrodite, why are you here, and with this mortal man too? Who is he and why is he here?' The questions were quick and succinct, with a hint of suspicion attached to them.

Peter appreciated the lovely vision, who caught his glance, and he detected a coy smile appear on her face.

Aphrodite took Andromeda's hand. 'Charon brought us to this land, for what purpose we do not know. We are looking for the soul of Adonis and this one's husband.' The disdain was back in her voice.

'Why here? This land has seen no mortal's soul in eons.' Andromeda was as confused as the others.

'The eye guided us. The boat we were travelling on steered us here.' Julie said.

'I see. And you believe the souls that you seek are here? Is that what the eye tells you?'

'Perhaps, but the only one who knows for sure is Persephone.' Aphrodite echoed the statement. 'She knows where the souls are kept.'

'Well, I hope you won't have a problem then, because she's not around. She is missing, disappeared a few days ago, but did not come here. Perhaps she is at Asphodel Meadows.'

'Why are we here then?' Aphrodite's question was directed at all of them.

'I suspect it's not to witness the tournament of the Carneia, which all the heroes are practicing for.' Andromeda motioned towards the arena below.

'It is odd that the eye wanted you to see this place as part of your odyssey.' Aphrodite said without looking at Julie. 'So far, you have witnessed the Underworld's desolation and seen some depravities. Maybe this part of the journey is to show you that you can still find beauty in ugliness.'

'But I need to find Richard?' Julie's words were tinged with a hint of sorrow.

'I wish I could help you more, but I have no words of comfort to share.' Andromeda continued. 'What I can say is that you must find Persephone because the red moon approaches. Hades will be in his element at this time and his power will be immense. Follow me,' she moved quickly, taking them down the hillside. 'I will take you back to the shore where Charon will be waiting. He cannot leave until he has completed taking you to journey's end, and this is not it.'

Rounding a corner, they were greeted by a magnificent white horse, whose head and mane were cloaked with a brilliant scarlet hood.

Andromeda pulled the cover from the horse's head and the animal reared slightly, its strong muscular legs kicking out as its hooves dug into the ground. She patted and soothed the beast as she moved to its rear and climbed onto an attached chariot which was the picture of supreme elegance with ornate and decorative carvings of heroic deeds etched into the body. And just as a Rolls Royce has its Spirit of Ecstasy as its emblem, the chariot had a figurine of Perseus brandishing his shield in the stance he used to defeat Medusa.

Peter stepped forward to look closer at the image.

'Ah, I see you are admiring my husband's bronze figure. It was carved by Myronas, the famous artist who made the bronze discus thrower, recognised now as a treasure of antiquity. Climb on, there is room for all three of you.'

The three clambered on board.

Andromeda took the reins and instead of using the whip against the horse, cracked it high in the air to encourage the animal to gallop away. She was a skilled charioteer, driving it with supreme flair as she swerved and twisted the two-wheel vehicle around bends and corners.

No one spoke, the adrenalin flowing through them at the excitement of the ride. As they sped through the Avenue of Heroes, the statues a mere blur.

Julie held tight to the chariot and even tighter to Peter's hand; there was more than friendship beginning to happen, they were bonding.

Chasing down the road flanked with cornfields, they passed a few inhabitants again in brief flashes. Then, as they rounded the last bend that led down to the shore, the horse slowed instinctively as it approached the multi-coloured curtain, and as the wheels rotated, it drew the chariot to a stop.

Andromeda climbed down first, followed by Aphrodite, then Julie and Peter. All four stood together, no one spoke; no words were needed. Aphrodite embraced Andromeda, kissing her on both cheeks in the age-old way of the Greeks.

Andromeda looked at Peter and Julie but did not offer her hand. Rather, she smiled and waved, then bid them a safe journey before climbing back on her chariot and leaving a trail of dust and the shadows of wheels in her wake.

Peter turned to his companions, 'Let's go,' and stepped forward into the curtain.

Charon, head bowed and still clothed in his filthy black garb, was tying the boat's rope to a wooden stump. Having just disembarked, he saw all three emerge through the curtain and step onto the shore. Groaning, he released the rope, his displeasure registering audibly when he mumbled to himself. 'When can I get rid of these fools?'

Peter climbed into the boat, and was quickly joined by the other two who like him now sported their shrouds again.

Julie took the eye in her hand and pointed it forward. The boat, now free, immediately moved in a direction, which was towards Asphodel Meadows.

25

THE GREYS

*H*ades was angry. He had learnt much from his encounter with the Moirai, but it was what he did not know that perplexed him the most. He needed confirmation of his best course of action, and the sisters Graeae, on the island of Cisthene, might have the answer.

These reclusive hags, a fitting description for a trio of what could be called blind women in the loosest sense, had but one tooth and a single eye between them. The very same eye that Perseus had taken from them to reveal the sanctuary of the Gorgon Medusa, who also was the Graeae's sister.

It was no longer about what had happened, but that he needed insight into the future and what he should do to protect his status quo.

It seemed like only a few minutes had passed since leaving *The Fates* but *Time*, as defined in the books of the world, did not apply to Hades; or rather, it worked only when it suited him. To this issue, the journey to Cisthene was timeless.

Suitably dressed again in another one of his most elaborate costumes fit only for a King, he set about seeking answers as he climbed up the jagged cliff edge.

The going was treacherous even for a god and he gingerly edged his way along the narrowest of paths before looking down to the crashing waves below. As he drew nearer to the top of the cliff, obnoxious smells emanated from a hole in the rock face that shocked him. Putrid and foul odours drifted around; the stench of rotting fish, flesh, and death. The last smell was one he was familiar with as it greeted him when he entered the inlet.

The entrance to the cave was rough. At its top were sharp pieces of rock that protruded outwards like sharp knives, perfectly honed to inflict the deepest of cuts. As he moved to avoid these jagged sentries, he saw the surface in front of him disappear.

Upon entering the cave, the inside was black and bereft of light. He put his hands against the wall and edged closer to where the foulest of all smells came from. It was at that point he heard the first voice.

'Come closer.'

Hades edged his way forward and a flicker of a light began twitching in the darkness.

'Closer.' The voice repeated, its message tinged with malevolence.

He could hear more voices now, cackling and laughter, which ran like an echo through the darkness.

Another voice interrupted, with a higher pitch than the first, and tinged with anxiety. 'Give me the eye, sister.'

Hades moved towards the light, snapping discarded bones under his feet. As he drew closer to the voices, they stopped. Fear was in reverse, for the eye had revealed who their visitor was.

Stepping out from the darkness and into the flame-lit cavern, Hades focussed on the three figures.

The first knelt, clasping the eye to her brow. 'My Lord, we are honoured by your presence.'

The two others joined their sister in tribute.

Hades said nothing, having already grown accustomed to the stench of the place and the sight of foul-looking things, because he had no words to describe their appearance. He had many minions in his domain that were just as bad as these creatures, but rarely did he come face-to-face with them as he was now. He moved deeper into the cave.

Putrid smells wafted about the place as if they had a life of their own, coming from rotting, indistinguishable animal carcasses that lay strewn across the floor. Small sharp pebbles lay before him, making walking even more precarious. Grim lighting from half-burnt candles kept vision to a minimum. Regardless, Hades distinguished between the three.

Seated at his right and sporting a large wooden stick with thorns protruding from its side was Deino, *The terrible*. Next to and seated slightly behind her was Enyo, her name meaning *warlike*. And finally, the one who seemed the most curious of the three, Pemphredo, *the one who guides the way*. Collectively, they were known as *The Grey Ones*, having been born that colour.

Hades stood, not daring to sit, and instead took his place beside Pemphredo.

She spoke while pointing a crooked finger in his direction and holding the eye to her brow. With this tool, she could focus directly on the god before them. 'You honour us with your presence, my Lord. How can we, as humble, unworthy, and degrading specimens be of service?'

Hades looked towards the voice, and the other two women drew closer to their sister. He crunched over the bones scattered in his path and took another step towards Pemphredo. 'It is not what you can do for me, wretches, it is what I am here to tell you.' He spoke with authority, sensing their subjugation. He commanded them. He was their Master.

'You bring us news, great Lord.' It was Deino's turn, the one who carried and supported herself with a stick as she rose from her awkward position clutching the eye to her head.

'The news concerns your sister…'

'Medusa.' Deino held the eye firmer.

'Yes, Medusa. We all know that the Gorgon's head has been kept secret for eons. Until now. For I have learned that my brother kept your sister's head secure in his birth cave; when we all thought it had been lost to the four winds. We know the power of the blood, how its richness can resurrect the dead. It was a prize I desired… no, craved, for it would have given me even greater powers which my brother would have hated. And for once, his omnipresence would have been tested fully and I would have been able to compete equally, or beat him. Her blood would have given me a distinct advantage, as I could have used it to resurrect an army of my own. This could have transpired, but the interference of a mortal, a woman no less… It is she who has stifled my plans.'

'Lord, how can this be? No mortal can challenge the gods.' Enyo's words resonated with Hades.

'That may be, Gray One, but this mortal has the support of my brother and he has given her the power of *perfect thought* and the eye. She used these to enter the cave where your sister's head was kept. I sent a manservant to follow her and eliminate her, but I have spoken with the Fates, and they tell me this woman has destroyed him.'

'Where is this mortal now, Lord?'

'I am told she is on her way to my Kingdom, the Underworld.'

The three sisters tried to grab the eye from each other, but Deino snatched it and held it to her head. 'I am trying to find her. The mist is not clearing and something is stopping me from seeing…'

'Give it to me, let me look.' Pemphredo grabbed the eye and repeated the process, lifting it to her forehead. She too could not see anything. 'Lord, we cannot see this woman of whom you speak. She is hidden, Lord.'

All three echoed the word 'Hidden.'

'The eye is keeping her from our gaze.'

'I came here to find out where she is now, but you tell me you cannot see her. You, with the power to find anyone, cannot see this mortal?' His voice rose in anger, his frustration boiling over.

Deino rose from the floor, shuffling across to kneel by Hades' feet, her crooked hand trying to stretch out to stroke his golden sandals. Looking up at the god standing above her, she spoke in a whisper, trying to appease him. 'She is but a mortal, Lord, she can offer you no threat. She will succumb to the Underworld and be lost forever. You have nothing to fear.'

'She destroyed my manservant. She can raise an army against me. She will take my Kingdom. Nothing to fear… you worthless hag.' Hades kicked out at the decrepit body, his foot aimed at her ribcage. As it broke the brittle bones in her body, his foot continued to lash out at the crumpled woman. 'Zeus wants my Kingdom, I am sure of it, and this mortal woman has given him the catalyst to do just that. It will be him who controls the purse strings in this treasure, not me. He alone brought this woman into my domain. I am the King of the Underworld, not him, yet through this woman, he seeks to infiltrate my Kingdom… Do you now understand what price is to be paid here?' His anger at fever pitch, he continued kicking her until she collapsed, and blood spurted across the floor.

The other two grabbed each other. Pemphredo took the eye, clutching it to her forehead. It showed her the beaten and bloodied body of her sister. 'What have you done?'

Hades stood unmoved by the pleading women.

'Leave now, do not return, you have created chaos where none was before. You have broken our bond with the gods, you have made us unbalanced.' The two sisters grabbed hold of their broken sister and cradled her in their arms.

Hades' parting words added more torment to the trio. 'I came here to tell you that your Gorgon sister is gone. She will never be heard of again. That mortal has seen to it.'

Bloodied and crushed, Deino rose slowly onto her knees. Turning her broken body towards him, her voice was weak. 'Leave.' It was just one word, but it meant defiance.

Hades walked away from the crumpled figure.

Echoing her sister's boldness, Pemphredo stood up and faced Hades. 'If what you say is true, then you should indeed fear this woman. Beware, Hades, her power is beyond your understanding if she has harnessed the power of *perfect thought* and it dwells in her. It will take more than you to destroy her.'

Hades looked down on the wretch lying on the floor, her breathing shallow. And it was at that moment that a thought entered his mind. 'Perhaps I won't have to.' He turned and edged his way through the cave.

Once outside, the air cleared and he found himself able to walk down the cliff edge easier than before. There was a new resolution about him as he edged his way down the narrow pathway, the sound of great waves crashing against the rocks below growing louder.

As he continued down the path, he mulled over what had transpired in the cave above. Was there a hint of remorse for his treatment of the old crone? No, that was not in his character. Sympathy and regret were words not in his vocabulary. His actions were always justified, whether right or not. His mind would not dwell on this any longer, he had more important things to do. But first, he needed to know where the mortal was and who was with her.

PERSEPHONE HAD HIDDEN HERSELF FROM HADES' clutches, knowing he would be looking for her. But she was cunning, for she knew not only the ways of the Labyrinth of the Underworld, but she knew how to get out. Once every two seasons, she visited the world above. This was the bargain she had struck with Hades.

She should be in the world above already, but she had promised Aphrodite that she would guide them out of the Underworld, should they succeed in their task.

How she missed the surface and yearned to return to it, to walk in the forests and bathe in the mountain streams. To sample the fruits and drink the wine. To become mortal again for just a few short days. She envied those who lived a mortal life, even though it meant their death, something she could only imagine. What that must be like to have eternal peace. It was a thought that occupied her mind a lot.

But for now, she had one pressing task to perform, find Aphrodite.

She left her sanctuary and made her way through the corridors of pain, towards Asphodel Meadows.

INSIDE THE UNDERWORLD

For those in the boat, it was difficult to comprehend just how far they had come. Was it still night or had they broken into a new day? Time was an expense they could not afford to lose, knowing that the blood-red moon would soon evolve and eclipse their efforts to free Richard. As the boat moved forward, they heard more mundane noises, conversations began, not screams of agony but real coherent words.

Unable to understand them, Julie turned to Aphrodite and whispered, 'Do you know what they are saying?'

'Yes. They are talking about a celebration the dead are taking part in and resenting the fact they are not included.'

'Is that it?'

'Yes. They complain that they want to go, but Hades has forbidden it. These spirits are ordinary, with no say in what happens to them, so they live their immortality in obscurity and in some way, serenity. This is something new to them, which is why they are upset.'

The boat slowed and pulled over to the side; the signal for them to get out. Aphrodite was first, followed by Julie, then

Peter, who was almost caught in the water as Charon pulled away before disappearing back into the mist.

On land, the two mortals and goddess made their way over a rocky pathway before emerging into a field full of flowers. Gingerly, they walked through the blooms. In front of them was what looked like an ancient settlement, typical Greek in its description, but with no grandiose pillars or temples just small little houses that lacked any design, plain and ordinary in keeping with the locals of the place. Locals who paid little attention to the newcomers. In fact, the best way to describe this whole place was ordinary, ordinary looking houses, ordinary looking streets, ordinary looking people save one abiding factor, they were all dead. Spirits who had done nothing to warrant any further accolade or recognition, but for those souls who had transgressed in their lives, would find themselves stuck in an afterlife of the ordinary.

Small hand-drawn carts with donkeys covered in the familiar green shroud plied their way through the narrow streets. Small trees and bushes decorated the surrounds. Asphodel Meadows showed no signs of the horror or terror they had been subjected to before.

As Aphrodite moved through the streets, the others followed, staring at the people, buildings, and the sheer lack of anything memorable. To the inhabitants, these new arrivals looked just the same as them.

'Hurry, she is here.' Aphrodite turned into a side street.

Standing at the end of a narrow alley was a beautiful woman, also shrouded in the green aura. She hurried across to Aphrodite, hugged and kissed her on the cheeks. Taking her hand, her eyes lit up, as she hugged her once again, before turning to Julie and Peter standing beside her. 'You must be Julie, Richard's wife.'

Julie nodded.

'We have all heard about you and your odyssey. No one gave

you a chance to make it this far… But here you are, with your companion.'

'My name is Peter.' He smiled at the woman who stood before them.

'I am Persephone, Hades' wife.'

She was a beauty. Her hair auburn, shoulder-length, and her face although bleach-white through the death aura, had a perfect complexion which highlighted almond-shaped dark-green eyes. She was taller than the other women, standing perfectly straight, as if a stick kept her shoulders square and supported her back. Even with the aura surrounding her, it was hard to take one's eyes from her.

'We have little time,' she said, 'I have learnt that your husband is in a building just around the corner and that soon, he will be prepared for his final hours, when he will then pass permanently into the Underworld. You must get him out before this happens, otherwise, he will be lost. But be quick, Hades is not far…' she looked over one shoulder. 'He is searching his domain, looking for me. So, you need to be swift before he returns. Do what you have to do, after which, I will get you out of here.

'Go down this street until you come to a large black door; it is not locked, go inside. The souls are kept in long containers, like caskets. The one you are searching for is red, as are the locks, but once they turn black, his soul is gone. Open the casket, use the eye I see you have around your neck, and *perfect thought*; I know Zeus taught you about that. With these two powers, you can release him. He will also be covered in a green aura, but not as vivid as yours, and he will not know you. Take him from the casket and bring him here as best you can. You may need to carry or drag him as he will be too weak to walk. Is that clear, do you understand?'

'Yes.' Julie said.

'Aphrodite, wait here with me, let the mortals bring the soul back.'

'What about Adonis?' Aphrodite urged.

'You will just have to wait.' Persephone said sharply then turned to Julie and Peter. 'Follow me, I will take you to the end of this road, then you are on your own. Remember, look for the red casket. There are thousands of souls in that place, but only a handful of red ones.'

'How will we know which one is Richard's?' Julie's anxious expression confirmed her worry.

'That is why you need *perfect thought* to find him, and the eye to open the casket. When done, return here, we will wait.' Persephone walked with them a short way down the road. 'Go now.'

Peter and Julie scanned the buildings ahead of them, and not more than fifty yards away was a building with a huge black door. They ran towards it. As they pushed the door open, a vast collection of caskets of all shapes and all sizes, which virtually lined the room from floor to ceiling, greeted them.

Julie fell to her knees, clutching the eye in one hand and holding the chalice in the other. 'Where are you, Richard? Help me find you!' Desperation crept into her voice as her eyes moved from box to box.

Peter ran up and down the long lines of coffins piled high and stacked in order. Feverishly, he checked the writing on them. All were in Greek or some script he could not read.

Gripping the eye in her hand, Julie prayed.

'*Perfect thought*, Julie, use it.' She could almost hear Zeus' words in her ear.

She stood up, held the eye in her hand, closed her eyes, cleared her mind of everything she knew, and concentrated on one thing only, the eye. She was beginning to understand *perfect thought* and its power seeping into her mind. She moved the caskets away in her mind, pushing them here and there, back and forth. As she cleared them from place to place, the one she was looking for came into focus. 'I see it, Peter, I see it.' She ran.

Peter followed, shouting. 'Where, where?'

'Here. This is it.' Julie gazed at a stack piled high with blue, green, purple, and yellow caskets. Right on top was a red one. She planted one foot on the bottom one and began the precarious climb. Holding the eye in her hand, she clambered up and up, then looked down onto the lid of the red one as it shone against the reflecting light. She waved the eye over the lid. The lock clicked and opened. She pulled the top off and it fell to the floor with a loud thud, narrowly missing Peter. She peered inside.

A mist floated from the casket and she could not see Richard, or anything else. She reached in, pushed her hands down, felt something clammy, and pulled whatever it was towards her as she balanced on the casket.

Peter stood below her, waiting to help.

As the vapour in the casket dissipated, she saw what she held in her hand and let out a scream before covering her mouth. 'Oh, my God. What has happened to you?'

Getting over the shock, she pulled the limp figure towards her. The only description going through her mind was that this poor creature looked like a desiccated human husk. He was naked, a translucent thin layer of skin covering his body, the face sunk back, and his eyes, deep in their sockets, looked as if they were about to drop out at any moment. His body was severely emaciated, all muscle gone. He felt as heavy as paper, and the faintest green aura surrounded him.

She leaned over to hold him with one hand whilst taking out the chalice. She opened it, checked to ensure that she had the right compartment, before pushing her fingers into Richard's mouth. It was difficult to open, but she could get it wide enough to pour the Gorgon's blood in his mouth. The liquid ran down from his lips, but some went into his throat. She waited.

Peter stood below, watching her hold her husband in her arms.

She looked at Richard, just skin and bones, no expression on his face. She prayed silently and put *perfect thought* in her mind, then leaned down to Peter, desperation showing on her face. 'Why is nothing happening?'

He looked for a way to climb up, without toppling the other coffins.

She put a hand up, halting him. 'Stay, he's breathing.' But her joy was short-lived. For as she tried to pick Richard up, she realised there was another body attached to him. It took her a second then she realised who it was. She shouted. 'Christ, Peter, there are two of them.'

Peter's expression was incredulous. 'How, why?'

'It must be Adonis. They are joined together, as one. Now, we don't have one to move, we have two. Thank God they are not heavy. But I do need your help. I just hope no one hears us.'

'What about the Gorgon's blood? Do you have enough for the other one?'

'I don't think I need it. Both of them are breathing, so it must have seeped through to him too.' She reached into the casket, dragging Richard out, and as she did so the attached figure of Adonis came with him.

Peter moved to the bottom of the caskets, awaiting Julie's careful descent to take both bodies as she reached him. The fact that they were weightless made everything much easier. He lay both spirits on the floor, where they stayed, motionless.

'We have to get them up and see if we can separate them. If not, we have to carry them back as they are.' Julie looked at Peter, a look of disbelief etched on her face.

'They're not heavy, I'll carry them. You just keep watching out for anybody or anything coming in.' Peter put Richard and the attached spirit of Adonis over one shoulder.

Julie pushed the black door open slowly to make their way

outside. Checking to see that all was clear, she motioned to proceed down the pathway and around the corner. It was surprisingly quiet, almost too quiet for a town, even a town of the dead.

'Oh, and what do we have here?' The voice was deep and menacing as it came echoing down the street.

27

HADES

The moment they had all dreaded was upon them.

Hades stood imperious in front of them, in his hand the leash that led to his favourite pet, Kerberos, the three-headed monster dog that snarled and licked its lips, showing its huge fangs and teeth. Hades snatched at the leash.

The hound lay down, its eyes focused on the new arrivals.

Hades' recent escapades had given him a new purpose, and it reflected in the dress he wore, which was no less regal than those he had travelled in. The velvet cloak and black boots, together with the gold belt around his waist, provided the perfect ensemble for royalty. The spectacle of superiority resonated from him. In this posture he looked at the minions assembled before him, dissecting each one with his razor-sharp eyes.

Their fear was obvious.

'Let me see,' he examined each of the new arrivals carefully, his eyes a brilliant shade of blue, and his facial expression dramatic. He strolled around them, scanning them as he moved. 'We have two mortals, a goddess, and… oh, a traitor wife. Hello, my darling, I wondered if I would find you mixed up with this. Did my brother put you up to it?'

'It was my idea, not his.' Aphrodite snapped back.

'Really. So, the goddess of Love has a thing for this mortal's spouse? Or is it that you want your lover back, who is so inconveniently stuck, if you excuse the expression, with the mortal?

And who might you be?' Hades turned his attention to Peter.

'I am a friend of the family.' Peter's reply was coy. His nerves would not let him say more.

'I see. So, that leaves you.' His glare fixed upon Julie. 'You must be JULIE, Richard's wife. The infamous mortal who dared to invade my Kingdom and whose idea it was to rescue your dead husband from my clutches?'

'It wasn't her idea, it was mine,' Aphrodite repeated.

'Silence. I will deal with you later, Daughter of Zeus.' Hades, turned his attention to Julie, almost mocking her. 'But perhaps if Aphrodite hadn't tried to seduce your husband in the first place and he had not succumbed to her charms, this would not have happened.'

Julie turned, realising the truth of Hades' statement. The ire growing inside her was about to burst, and goddess or no goddess, she was going to let her have it. 'He is right, we wouldn't be here if it wasn't for you. Richard would still be with me if you hadn't interfered in our life. You are the reason he is dead.'

'Ladies, please. And as much as I love a good cat fight, I don't have time.' He raised his voice and the town reverberated to the sound. 'I decide what goes on here, not you, these mortals, or my wife. Me, do you understand?' He turned his attention to the two spirts lying lifeless on the ground. 'Now, what are we to do with these poor souls?' He flicked his boot at Richard's body and it almost went through him. 'See how frail they are? Mere shadows of the men they once were. There's nothing left, and I believe it would be kinder for both to continue their transition to the Underworld. Poor devils.' He grinned as he watched the expressions of the others gathered around him.

'Please, Lord Hades, give me back my husband.' Julie fell to her knees, her face on the god's boot. 'Return Richard to me.'

'Such devotion, and this from the mortal who had no compunction in sending my servant to the afterlife. Yes, I know all about your little escapade in Zeus' Cave. How you used the Gorgon's head to destroy him. Clever little thing, aren't we? And, Mr Peter had a hand in this too.'

Both mortals stood silently.

'What about you, Aphrodite? What a treasure you would make for this world, and I am sure you would feel right at home here. I could even arrange for you to have conjugal visits with Adonis. Because, my dear sweet niece, as they say in Hotel California, you can check in any time you like, but you can never leave. I always loved that band.' Hades bristled with the alacrity of his position. 'I am sure my brother would not miss you, as you always seem to cause him so much worry. And what of you, my love?' He looked straight at his wife. 'How and when did you arrange this? And what a coincidence and how convenient that I should be away as you twisted your little web of deceit. Don't I give you everything your heart desires? All I ask for in return is a little company, six months of the year, to warm my body in the cold winter months.'

'You did not seduce me, like you tell everyone. You raped me.' Persephone confronted her husband.

'And you have betrayed me, so I think we are even now. But just in case you were thinking of running away with these mortals, let me show you where you will end up if you ever disobey me again.' Hades stood bolt upright and waved one hand twice, once to the right and the second to the left. 'This, my love, is where you will go.'

As the four stood together they felt their bodies rise above the ground. Hades moved his hand forward and they observed a place so desolate, so devoid of spirit and intensely evil that the vibrations felt under their feet made the ground give way. They fell, tumbling past one fragmented and tortured soul to the next. Their descent into Hell a ride of sheer terror, as face by tortured face became mirrored in their reflection. The smell of burning and a thick black smoke assaulted their senses, making their eyes bleed as they dropped further and further into the abyss. Where the flames rose highest, intense cold bit its way through their bodies, the contrast between sheer heat and intense cold no different. Both elements the prelude to what still lay ahead.

A snippet in time turned into minutes that felt like hours. As she stared down a long corridor, Julie found herself alone. She looked around for the others, but there was no sign of them. Slowly, she walked on. It was a long corridor, without rooms or decoration, that cast no shadows, the only light coming from a glass chandelier looming over her. She continued walking, looking for signs of the others' presence. She hesitated and stopped, looking straight down the corridor into a vast glass mirror at the end of the passageway. She drew closer and gazed at her reflection; her face was tired and drawn, her eyes sad, her expression one of loss.

Behind her, Hades cast his own reflection.

The mirror misted over before it cleared, and she stood staring at the figures inside. As they emerged, the reflections developed definition. Peering into the glass, her children's familiar faces came into view. They were driving in Matthew's car, relaxed and happy. Julie had not seen her kids since she had left, which seemed a lifetime ago.

Hades stepped closer. "Mrs Cole, there are all kinds of Hell. Some...' he touched the glass, 'some are brought upon by the deeds we weave in our troubled waters. Others are...'

Julie stood resolute, staring into the mirror. Matthew's car was turning onto a major road when a huge truck hit them head on. She fought to control her tears and emotions, because if she showed one sign of weakness now, she would be finished. She gripped the eye and prayed for *perfect thought*. The strength returned to her as she struggled to keep her children from her mind. She must keep them away from Hades' grip.

'Accidental. Either way, the outcome is the same.' Hades looked deeply into the mirror.

Julie stared back at him and the images began to fade. The battle was almost tangible as god fought mortal.

Hades sensed her pain but the more he tried to drag it from her, the stronger her *perfect thought* became. 'My brother has taught you well.' He walked away, mulling his thoughts over in his mind. 'The power of *perfect thought* together with a mother's love is something I have never known.' There was melancholy in those words. Dismissing the thought instantly, he turned to her again. 'We shall return, for there is much to ponder.'

Julie was desperate to sob her heart out, but she needed to pick her place.

The others stood beside Hades, their own slice of Hell complete.

'Now, let us dispense with this little show.' He waved his hand again.

They were back in Asphodel Meadows, everything back in its rightful place.

'I think you can all appreciate my point of view now. Only I control this place, as I have proven to you in your own little vignettes that I prepared for your pleasure. Moving on to more pressing matters. The blood moon will soon rise, so if you have not left my world by the time it does, both poor creatures will be mine. Suggestions, anybody?'

The two spirits lay on the ground, barely breathing.

'Aphrodite, no ideas? You, the goddess of Love, can't give me a reason to save your lover? What about you, Mrs Cole? heroine of the day, what of your darling Richard? Surely you couldn't have done all this for nothing? you must have a plan.' Hades walked among them then turned back to Julie. 'I am disappointed, Mrs Cole. Or may I call you Julie? Yes, Julie, I am surprised. But perhaps dazed is a better word to use, by your lack of response. Or is that all you were expecting to happen? You would find Richard, rescue his soul, and be reunited with him? And then what? What did you think would happen then? That suddenly, he would be whole again? That he would be free from my clutches? Is that what you thought was going to happen?' Hades' smile was one of sarcasm. 'No, Julie, the Underworld does not work like that. I don't work like that. Or perhaps you expected Persephone to lead you back into your world, where Richard would be as he was. Is that what you thought?'

Julie stood motionless.

'No, Mrs Cole. After the inconvenience you have put me through, taking my man from me, and destroying my plans, it is inconceivable to just let you go. But I concede, like you, and I too am at a loss to know what to do next. I know what I should do, but I also have some respect for you, because what you have done will be talked about in our realm for decades. But although I respect you, I am still bound by my honour to chastise you.'

Julie knelt by her husband, stroking his hair and face, trying to ignore the harsh words.

Hades looked around at the defeated faces as they sat on the ground, blank expressions of hopelessness evident. 'None of you has a solution? I am disappointed. Well, it looks like I will take these two back to their caskets.'

'Excuse me, Lord Hades,' Peter stepped forward. 'Might I make a suggestion? But in private.'

'I am listening, mortal.'

'In private, please.' Peter insisted.

'I do not give audiences, and certainly not to mortals.'

'Please, Lord Hades, I believe you will find my proposal appealing and worthy of your status.'

'I am intrigued by your persistence. Walk this way. I will blot out the ears of the others, so you can speak freely.'

It was the strangest of sights, to the point of being surreal.

The *Lord of the Dead* walking with an ex-helicopter pilot. Upon reaching a convenient spot, Hades sat down.

Peter, respecting his position and not wanting to rock the boat, stood, then nodded and stepped a little away from him. 'Thank you, Lord Hades. My idea is quite simple and I believe you will like it. But I have one condition, which you must agree to.'

'I do not agree to anything unless it suits me and you are in no position to dictate terms. I set the terms; you understand me?' Hades' eyes focussed on the man. Was it courage or just blind stupidity that brought him here?

Peter looked down at the god. Although terrified by his demeanour, it also gave him a great sense of purpose and an odd feeling of superiority, which, in the presence of a god, was hard to achieve.

Hades listened to the proposal, his eyes following the man's movements as he spoke, and a sly grin graced his lips. Then he sat a minute, running the entire idea over in his mind again. He stood up and Peter bowed his head.

Peter thought about offering his hand, but changed his mind, and kept two steps behind before they returned to the others, who all stood waiting anxiously.

'Well, let it not be said that a god cannot be surprised and shocked by mere mortals. Now, we have a decision on what to do next. Mr Shaw has put forward a good proposition, which I am in favour of. Also, we can dispense with these death shrouds, I believe we all know who we are.' As he spoke the green auras vanished from their bodies and he could better pick out Julie's features distinctly; he appreciated her figure and looks. 'I am glad we got rid of those, you could all have caught your deaths, excuse the pun. As I was saying, Mr Shaw has an admirable plan, which will help answer the question of who stays.'

'What do you mean who stays?' Aphrodite's question was to the point.

'My dear sweet niece, surely you know by now that I am not charitable. Your father wasn't very charitable either when he cast lots for who should rule where. I drew the shortest straw and got this place. For me, charity begins at home.'

'What do you propose then?' Aphrodite asked again.

'This is not my idea but Mr Shaw's.' Hades clapped twice, in a symbolic gesture of appreciation. 'Very good, Mr Shaw.' He turned, and what looked like a smile slowly formed across his somewhat contented face.

28

THE PROPOSAL

*H*ades stood with the others. If the situation and location had not been so weird and extreme it could almost pass for an ordinary day. But this was no ordinary place, and the people were not normal. There was no normality in this environment. How could there be? The dead do not go well with the living, regardless of their circumstances.

As they waited on a pavement of the nondescript dead town, Hades and his monster dog moved up and down the street.

Julie turned to Peter and whispered. 'What have you agreed with him?' When he didn't react, she pinched his arm.

'Ow, stop that. You'll find out soon enough, he's just pondering over my suggestion again, trying to work out if there is a catch. But it will be fine, I promise.' Peter squeezed her hand.

Hades returned, looked at his wife, then Aphrodite, and finally at the two mortals. 'It is an excellent plan, Mr Peter, I am agreed that this is what we will do. First, I need to release these two from their death trance. Afterwards, we will travel to the place you suggested, and there conduct your experiment. Actually, I am looking forward to it. Persephone, I leave you in charge while I'm gone, do nothing rash or stupid. I shall return as soon as possible.'

Persephone bowed her head. 'Yes, my husband.'

'What about me?' Aphrodite stood up and spoke directly to Hades.

'You, my special niece, are to come with me and the others.'

'Where?'

'Why, where it all began.' Hades leered a glance at the goddess. 'Your birthplace, Petra Tou Romiou.'

She looked perplexed and probed. 'Why there?'

'Because it is fitting for what I have in mind. Enough now, we will explain more when we get there.'

Richard and Adonis stirred, their bodies starting to fill as if they were inhaling air into them. Their faces lost the pallor of death, coming alive as blood began flowing through their veins and their muscles grew. Hair that had become limp and dirty took on a new vibrancy, and eyes that were shallow and sunken, were wide open and shining. Life was once again inside their bodies and the two souls separated.

Richard was the first to react. He stood up, looked at those gathered around him, and did not recognise anyone.

Aphrodite stepped forward, grabbed hold of Adonis, and screamed at Hades. 'What have you done to him, why is he like that?'

'What did you expect from someone who has been dead for almost a year? His spirit has been held in a cocoon between life and death. He and your husband, Mrs Cole, have been between worlds. That is the easiest way to explain it. Now, they are free from that bondage, but are still not ready to respond, not until they are normal again.'

'When will that be?'

'Soon. Now, that's it.' Hades was adamant that enough explanations had been made as his temper rose sharply. 'Wait here, all of you, I have things to do.' He took Kerberos by the leash and walked away, leaving the others pondering on his next move.

Peter took Julie by the arm. 'Come with me. I want to ask you something.'

The two mortals walked a distance down the street, passing the occasional spirit beings. They stood outside a small shop. It was a clothes store. In the windows were images of men and women clothed in their shrouds. It would appear that shrouds were the fashion of the day.

'What is it, Peter?'

'I don't know how to say this, as it has been playing on my mind for a while.'

'What is it?'

'One way or another, you will have Richard back, but how will you explain to the kids that their father is not dead? Where did you find him and how did you bring him back?' Peter's expression was one of pure curiosity.

'I don't know. Did I ever think we would get this far? In my heart of hearts I believed we could, but my senses told me we never would. But with your help we could it became possible. Now, I have the real chance to bring Richard home, I just don't know how to do it. I have wondered about this on and off too. Ever since we left Zeus' cave I have asked myself, *what if we actually resurrect him? what happens then?* So, what do I do now?'

'Only you know that answer, Jules. But you've come this far, so I'm sure you will figure it out.' He planted a small kiss on her cheek.

In the domain of the dead, this was a symbol of love.

Julie looked into his eyes, smiled, and realised he was more than a friend. But she had done so much more than that, she had also kept her children from Hades' influences. She still had no idea what had happened to them, the image in the mirror taunting her, but first, she must get Richard back. Only then could she look for the answers to her questions.

29

ALPHA AND OMEGA

It was altogether fitting that the place where it all began should be the place where it would end.

The parties gathered on the beach at Petra Tou Romiou in a line that snaked along the shore, but of all the characters that stood on the beach, Hades shocked those standing with him the most. He had reverted to his Necromancer image and become the decrepit figure who had held court in London, instead of the regal look that he carried off so well in the Underworld. Not only was he dishevelled-looking, but his facial features had changed to that of an old man, with sunken cheekbones, bloodshot eyes, and an emaciated body.

His clothing was loose-fitting and far too big for his frame. He wore the distinctive, vivid red jacket and black trousers, which were rolled up into his long black boots. His breathing was slow and shallow, but his voice was still commanding and guttural.

Aware of his appearance, he shuffled his frame among those awaiting his next words. 'Forgive my somewhat shabby appearance.' He said, as if apologising, though a gleam never left his eyes. 'But this is how I look when I come to the surface, as my age comes with me. In my capacity as Lord of the Dead, it is necessary when I meet with my followers to show them how time has treated me, which is why they never question my divinity or power. I may look frail and useless, but even in this pathetic form I still have dominion over them, as I do over you, so never doubt what you see before you.' His affirmation of supremacy quickly reinforced in those words. 'Ah, good, the blood moon is almost at its zenith. We must begin.'

The waters of Petra Tou Romiou moved, as if being stirred by some giant whisk. Enormous waves formed and rushed onto the shore faster and faster, each one growing larger with every wake.

'It is time.' Hades stepped forward, shuffled to the water's edge, bent down, and dipped his fingers in the waves as they sped ashore. It was an effort. 'Yes, this will do.' He turned towards his somewhat baffled onlookers. 'Now, you may be asking yourselves why we are gathered here. The answer is simple, Alpha and Omega. For those not familiar with the Greek words, it means the beginning and the end, which I see as this…' he stretched his hands out towards the waves, 'and the answer to my dilemma. One of these two will return to me, the other will stay with their loved one. Normally, that would be a simple choice. Adonis would be the victor with his superior strength and godlike qualities. But, and this is difficult for me to admit.' He turned to face Julie. 'You beat me, Mrs Cole, to the Gorgon's blood. No easy task for any god, let alone a female mortal. No, Mrs Cole, I recognise your courage and tenacity and find your husband worthy of a concession, or, call it a reward. Which is why I have given your husband the same power as Adonis. To make the trial fair.'

'That is generous of you, my brother.'

Hades turned.

Zeus strode through the purple cloud curtain down to the beach to stand next to Julie.

'Well, well, my little brother has come to see me. Or is it someone else you came to see? Perhaps Mrs Cole?'

'You never change, do you? Must you always look for an ulterior motive?' Zeus remonstrated. 'But yes, I came to see Mrs Cole. I also came to make sure that whatever you are planning is done fairly. She deserves that.'

'You need not have bothered, the plan was in fact concocted by Mr Peter here. He came up with the idea, so there is no need for you to be involved.'

The two gods eyed each other, both vying for supremacy of the situation. Looking directly at Hades, Zeus conceded that he was only an observer, that he would not use his powers to influence the outcome.

'Your daughter believes Adonis will be the champion. Personally, I would put the mortal as the favourite, as I am sure every deity in and outside of Olympus already prefers Mr Cole to be the winner.'

Julie stepped forward, nodding to Mr Christoulides. Should she have bowed instead? Perhaps not, even though she was dying to tell him about her odyssey and what she had done. But that would be for another time. Now, she had to channel her *perfect thought* to Richard.

The two spirits stood by the water's edge. It would be wrong to call them men, as essentially, they were still dead, even though their bodies appeared to be alive.

'As you can see, the waters are awakening. All of you are familiar with this place and the living legend, which says your true love will be revealed after three circuits around Aphrodite's rock. Today, that legend takes on a new meaning; the victor will take home the spoils.' Hades pointed out to sea before he turned to the competitors. 'The two of you will swim around that rock three times, and at the end, whoever wins will remain here, whilst the other returns with me to the Underworld.'

Aphrodite moved forward. 'Come back to me, Adonis.' She urged and kissed him on the lips.

Taking a few steps towards the bemused figure of her husband, Julie took the eye from her neck and placed it around his. She too kissed her husband on the lips gently.

Both spirts took off their clothes, standing naked before gods and mortals.

'Three times around that rock.' Hades put three fingers up, making sure both understood, then turned to Aphrodite. 'Take that silk from around your neck and drop it on the ground. It will be the signal for the race to start.'

Looking directly into Hades' eyes, Aphrodite removed the piece of silk, held it high above her head, and let it drop. It fluttered for less than three seconds before hitting the shore.

Richard and Adonis ran into the water, the breakers beating hard upon their bodies. The race for the second chance at life had begun. Richard swam well and was a few strokes ahead of Adonis who fought against the waves as they swept over his naked body. The further they got from shore battling the elements, the more the voices screaming words of encouragement faded.

Overhead, the blood moon shimmered and cast a dazzling reflection across the surf. Richard felt the waves crash against him as he rounded the rock for the first time, and Adonis pushed his spirit-body harder to reach the same level. As they got closer to shore the voices from the crowd grew louder, all shouting incoherent words.

The second lap saw Adonis sprint ahead of Richard.

Aphrodite screamed from the shore, her feet immersed in the water, urging Adonis on.

Peter held onto Julie, who couldn't bear to look, as the gap grew bigger and Adonis moved away. To comfort her, he put his arm around her and held her tight. He could almost sense her tears, which were ready to flow knowing that Richard would not make it.

Adonis rounded the Rock and left Richard in his wake.

Aphrodite stood in the water, clapping her hands, and screaming 'yes, yes,' knowing Julie was listening to her screams of delight.

The gap between them was now four lengths.

Hades rubbed his hands together.

Zeus looked away. It would appear that all of Julie's efforts and her odyssey were in vain, she was losing Richard.

Adonis slowed, his energy sapping from him, while Richard was catching up, but there were less than thirty meters to go.

As they rounded the rock for the third time, the energy and excitement from Aphrodite was almost tangible as she yelled and screamed at Adonis, who was fading fast.

Richard was only two lengths from him now, with the distance to the Rock about the same, every muscle, sinew, and joint in his spirit-body pushed harder and faster to catch up, but although Adonis was fading, there was no way to catch him.

Julie moved away from Peter and down to the water's edge, where she sank to her knees, her eyes focused on her husband as the last minutes of his life with her ended.

Adonis reached the Rock the winner.

Aphrodite jumped, shouted, and gloated. 'You see, mortal, gods win. We win because we are immortal and invincible, and I have washed away your efforts to claim back your husband in my birthplace.'

The two swimmers floated on the water, exhausted.

Hades moved across to the shore, looked out to the distant figures, and raised his hand to move them forward. He stopped as the two spirits tread water together, both looking towards the gathered assembly at the shore.

Aphrodite called to Adonis to go to her, whilst Julie stood up to say her last goodbye. The moon was full and blood red.

As those ashore waited for the two competitors to return, they watched as Adonis breathing heavily moved to the shore and then towards Richard.

Hades slithered forward, unable to contain the grin that swept across his face. 'Well, that was fun.'

Adonis turned and vanished, taking Richard with him.

LIKE THE OTHERS on the beach, Zeus stood silent. Even with all his omnipotence, he was still powerless to stop the events or interfere. Instead, he walked across to Julie and held her hand. 'When you're ready to leave, Pegasus is waiting to take you two back home, all arrangements have been made. I am sorry this did not work out for you, Julie, but your bravery and courage will become a legend in the annals of our history. May your God bless you, as I bless you. This is the last time we will see each other, and that is something I regret. Now, I must speak to my daughter.'

Holding back the tears, Julie kissed the mighty Zeus' hand and watched as he walked over to the jubilant Aphrodite.

'What did I tell you Father? Adonis won. These mortals are no match for the power of the gods.'

'Daughter, all decisions have consequences. Yes, Adonis won the race but your decision to use the Scylla and wreak havoc across this island must be paid for whether you are a god, goddess, or mortal. Adonis is beyond reproach; he is not guilty of anything and will spend his time in Olympus, but for you there is a different outcome. So, I have decided that you will see him only once every 366 days. Adonis will return to Olympus, whilst you will be left alone. This is your fate now, to live a life of solitude and to be forever more *Mistress of the Rock*.' He walked away.

'No, Father, no, he won.' Aphrodite lay on the beach, her face covered by tears and sand.

Peter took Julie's hand and they too walked away from the beach, up the hill, towards the purple curtain that separated the gods from their world.

Julie felt the tears run down her face. 'Oh, Peter, I have lost him. What am I to do?'

'You didn't lose him.'

She stopped and looked at Peter, it was his face and body but this was not his voice.

He smiled and nodded. 'Yes, it is me, Richard. It is Peter's body, but it's my spirit inside him. But only you will know. You and Hades.'

'What?' Julie, stunned and mesmerised, looked at the man standing in front of her. He looked like Peter, but it was not him, his whole personality was Richard's.

'This was the agreement Peter made with Hades to set me free. I will live in his body, he in mine, and he will stay in the Underworld in Elysium with the heroes and heroines. He told me how you saved him when I first came out of the casket, whispered it in my ear as he carried me back. He wasn't sure whether I heard him, but I did, and that's when he told me how much he was indebted to you. He also told me how his mortal life was a shambles, and how you had gone through so much to bring me back. The sacrifice to give up his own life for you was worth it. So, he made this bargain with Hades.'

'Oh my God, Richard, it really is you.' She threw her arms around her husband.

To the outsider, it might have looked strange how close the two had become so quickly, but only they knew the secret no one else would ever suspect.

'What do we tell the kids?' Julie smiled as she hugged her husband.

'Tell them you and I, Peter, became close, so close you fell in love with me. I mean, we were all over this place and this is The Island of Love. I hear people do it all the time over here.'

'Oh, Peter… I mean, Richard, you have an answer for everything.'

'Yes. Now, where is that plane we are supposed to get on?'

As they climbed the hill, the purple curtain disappeared, and they found themselves back on the roadside. Cars passed them by as they crossed the road, but waiting inside the parking area was a black taxi. Both climbed in the back, holding each other's hand as they sat down.

'Airport, sir?' The taxi driver did not turn around.

'Yes, then, home.' Julie interrupted, as she leaned forward, then looking in the driver's mirror, she smiled.

It would appear that Hermes was now a taxi driver.

THE RETURN

$\mathcal{I}$t took a while for the Cole children to grasp what had happened to their mother and accept their step-father in waiting. But as days passed, the heavy gloom that had dominated their lives for the past year lifted.

It was the perfect arrangement for Julie. By day, Peter was her man, but when she snuggled down in bed, it was Richard who lay beside her. If people only knew. She had created her own perfect 'Ménage et Trois.'

For Aphrodite, where she had once been recognised as the *sacred feminine*, her life was now an empty shell, as empty as the one Botticelli had painted. Her kingdom was only hers, as it was the day she was born.

Often, at night, she wandered the shoreline lamenting her lost lover. Rarely seen as more than the ephemeral spirit of the place, a mist or a silent wind, brushing the tops of the waves as they cascaded towards the rocks.

Why on this one particular night she let herself be seen, is a question only she can answer.

~

Petra Tou Romiou, October 2013

Actual Statement:

'I was with friends on the beach; it was pitch black, we could only see with our flashlights and what little light there was from the moon.

We noticed something moving on the top of the hill. At first, we thought it was just a tall bin, however; it turned out we were wrong.

Two friends and I walked up the hill to take a closer look.

It was a woman around 18-27 years old, from what I could tell from her body type, she was barefooted, wearing a white dress just past her knee. Her hair was long and it looked wet and covered her face. We spoke to her in Greek and in English but no response; we kept walking towards her until we were about two metres from her. She never moved, we got scared there was something not right and we walked away. She stayed there for about thirty minutes. We went back to the beach.'

As witnessed by,

Riz Nasir – Kris Brigilis – Alex Palzon – Panayoti Savvides

THE END

ABOUT THE AUTHOR

Born in 1952 in Orsett, Essex in England, the youngest son to Welsh parents Iris and Bill Edwards. Upon leaving school, he went into the travel industry, where he travelled the world, working in travel agencies, tour operators and airlines for some 30 years.

In 1976 Myron began freelance writing for BBC, radio and television, his credits include The Two Ronnies, Week Ending, and The News Huddlines. In 1980, he joined JWT advertising, as a copywriter writing his first TV commercial for dog food inside 10 days.

His love for the creative never left him and in 1987 he created Tubewalking, a new map concept, to help people get around London easier on foot, which still operates today.

In 1990 he married Niki, whose family background is Greek Cypriot. On a family trip to Cyprus, visiting Aphrodite's Rock for the first time, the beginnings of his passion to write the story of Mistress of the Rock came into fruition.

Moving his family in 2005 to Cyprus to live, gave him the opportunity to write, as during this time he worked on campaigns for TV and Radio in an advertising agency in Limassol.

The first manuscript of the book was completed in 2007, released by a local publisher it had a limited audience, but was well received by those who had read it. He has now completed the sequel and is working on the third part of this story.

Myron has three children, two sons and one daughter all grown up.